T4-APR-552

SCIENCE
FICTION

Halloween Horrors

Also by Alan Ryan

QUADRIPHOBIA
CAST A COLD EYE
DEAD WHITE
THE KILL
PANTHER!

Edited by Alan Ryan

NIGHT VISIONS 1
PERPETUAL LIGHT

Halloween Horrors

EDITED BY
ALAN RYAN

DOUBLEDAY & COMPANY, INC.
GARDEN CITY, NEW YORK
1986

All of the characters in this book
are fictitious, and any resemblance
to actual persons, living or dead,
is purely coincidental.

Library of Congress Cataloging-in-Publication Data

Halloween horrors.

Contents: He'll come knocking at your door/by
Robert R. McCammon—Eyes/by Charles L. Grant—
The Nixon mask/by Whitley Strieber—[etc.]
1. Halloween—Fiction. 2. Horror tales, American.
3. Horror tales, English. I. Ryan, Alan, 1943– .
PS648.H22H35 1986 813'.0872'0833 86-4460
ISBN: 0-385-19558-3

Printed in the United States of America
First Edition

This book is dedicated to
PAT LoBRUTTO
who knows a nasty idea when he hears it

Contents

Introduction: "Halloween Night"
by Alan Ryan

Halloween night is so damp and so chill,
a night of black evil, a night of cold ill,
it's dark in the evening,
then darker still,
on Halloween, Halloween night.

Halloween night is the one night to dread,
a night for all spirits to feed and be fed,
and to dance and to prance
on the night of the dead,
on Halloween, Halloween night.

Halloween night is a bonfire that's bright,
with a flame that's a friendly and flickering light,
until ghostly spirits
float into your sight,
on Halloween, Halloween night.

Halloween night is a pumpkin that grins,
to protect you from goblins who'll stick you with pins,
but when you are dead
it's the goblin who wins,
on Halloween, Halloween night.

Halloween night is the night to beware,
for ghosts are dishonest and goblins unfair.
So face them and fight them, my child,
if you dare,
on Halloween, Halloween night.

Halloween Horrors

Introduction:

He'll Come Knocking at Your Door

BY ROBERT R. MCCAMMON

Robert R. McCammon is a personable and easy-going fellow who lives in Birmingham, Alabama. His first four novels, all published as paperback originals, won him a wide following: *Baal, Bethany's Sin, The Night Boat,* and *They Thirst.* That last one is a particularly wild and colorful romp of a horror novel, with everything from a crazed albino motorcyclist to a mad mortician. Since then, his novels include the well-received *Mystery Walk* and *Usher's Passing,* which chronicles the dark lives of the descendants of Poe's fictional family.

McCammon seldom writes short stories. For this one he draws on his Southern background to take us—on the darkest night of the year—into the Deep South. Very deep indeed.

He'll Come Knocking at Your Door

BY ROBERT R. MCCAMMON

In the Deep South, Halloween Day is usually shirt-sleeve weather. But when the sun begins to sink, there's a foretaste of winter in the air. Pools of shadow deepen and lengthen, and the Alabama hills are transformed into moody tapestries of orange and black.

When Dan Burgess got home from the cement plant in Barrimore Crossing, he found Karen and Jaime working over a tray of homemade candies in the shape of pumpkins. Jaime, three years old and as curious as a chipmunk, was in a hurry to try out the candy. "Those are for the trick-or-treaters, hon," Karen explained patiently for the third or fourth time. Both mother and daughter were blond, though Jaime had inherited Dan's dark brown eyes. Karen's eyes were as blue as an Alabama lake on a sunny day.

As Dan hugged his wife from behind and peered over her shoulder at the candies, he felt a sense of satisfaction that made life seem deliciously complete. He was a tall man, his face lean and rugged from hard outdoor labor. He had curly dark brown hair and a beard in need of trimming. "Looks pretty Halloweeny around here, folks!" he drawled, and lifted Jaime into his arms when she reached up for him.

"Punkins!" Jaime said gleefully.

"Hope we get some trick-or-treaters tonight," Dan said. "Hard to tell if we will or not, this far from town." Their home, a rented two-bedroom farmhouse set off the main highway on a couple of acres of rolling woodland, was part of a subdivision of Barrimore Crossing called Essex. The business district of Barrimore Crossing was four miles to the east, and the thirty-five or so inhabitants of the Essex community lived in houses similar to Dan's, comfortable places surrounded by woods where deer, quail, possum, and fox were common sights. At night, Dan could sit on his front porch and see the distant porch lights of other Essex houses up in the hills. It was a quiet, peaceful place. And lucky too, Dan knew. All sorts of good things had happened to them since they'd moved here from Birmingham, after the steel mill shut down in February.

"Might have a few." Karen began to make eyes in the pumpkins with little silver dots of candy. "Mrs. Crosley said they always have a group of kids from town. If we didn't have treats for them, they'd probably egg our house!"

"Hallo'een!" Jaime pointed excitedly toward the pumpkins, wriggling to be set down.

"Oh, I almost forgot!" Karen licked a silver dot from her finger and walked across the kitchen to the cork bulletin board next to the telephone. She took off one of the pieces of paper stuck there by a blue plastic pin. "Mr. Hathaway called at four." She gave him the note, and he sent Jaime down. "He wants you to go over to his place for some kind of meeting."

"Meeting?" Dan looked at the note. It said *Roy Hathaway. His house, 6:30.* Hathaway was the real estate agent who'd rented them this house. He lived across the highway, up where the valley curved into the hills. "On Halloween? Did he say what for?"

"Nope. He did say it was important, though. He said you were expected, and it was something that couldn't be explained over the phone."

Dan grunted softly. He liked Roy Hathaway, who'd bent over backward to find them this place. Dan glanced at his new Bulova wristwatch, which he'd won by being the thousandth person to buy a pickup truck from a dealership in Birmingham. It was almost five-thirty. Time enough for a shower and a ham sandwich, and then he'd go see what was so important. "Okay," he said. "I'll find out what he wants."

"Somebody'll be a clown by the time you get back," Karen said, glancing slyly at Jaime.

"Me! Me'll be a clown, Daddy!"

Dan grinned at her and, his heart full, went back to take his shower.

Darkness was falling fast as Dan drove his white pickup truck along the winding country road that led to Hathaway's place. His headlights picked out a deer as it bolted in front of the truck.

Beyond the ridge of hills to the west, the setting sun tinted the sky a vivid orange.

Meeting, Dan thought uneasily. What was it that couldn't wait? He wondered if it might have something to do with the last rent check. No, no; his days of rubber checks and irate landlords were over. There was plenty of money in the bank. In August, Dan had received a letter that said they'd won five thousand dollars in a contest at the Food Giant store in Barrimore Crossing. Karen didn't even recall filling out an entry slip. Dan had been able to pay off the new truck and buy Karen the color television she'd been wanting. He was making more money than ever before, since his promotion in April from gravel-shoveler to unit supervisor at the cement plant. So money wasn't the problem. What was, then?

He loved the Essex community. It was fresh air and bird songs and a low-lying morning mist that clung like lace in the autumn trees. After the smog and harshness of Birmingham, after the trauma of losing his job and being on unemployment, Essex was a gentle, soul-soothing blessing.

Dan believed in luck. In hindsight, it was even good luck that he'd lost that job at the mill, because if he hadn't he never would have found Essex. One day in May he'd walked into the hardware and sporting goods store in Barrimore Crossing and admired a double-barreled Remington shotgun in a display case. The manager had come over, and they'd talked about guns and hunting for the better part of an hour. As Dan had started to leave, the manager unlocked that display case and said, Dan, I want you to try this baby out. Go ahead, take it! It's a new model, and the Remington people want to know how folks like it. You take it home with you. Bring me back a wild turkey or two, and if you like that gun tell other folks where they can buy one, hear?

It was amazing, Dan thought. He and Karen were living some kind of fantastic dream. The promotion at the plant had come right out of the blue. People respected him. Karen and Jaime were happier than he'd ever seen them. Just last month, a woman Karen had met at the Baptist church gave them a rich harvest of garden vegetables that would last them through the autumn. The only remotely bad thing that had happened since they'd moved to Essex, Dan recalled, was when he'd made a fool of himself in Roy Hathaway's office. He'd sliced his finger on the edge of a piece of paper and had bled all over the lease. It was a stupid thing to remember, he knew, but it had stuck in his mind because he'd hoped it wasn't a bad omen. Now he knew nothing could be further from the truth.

He rounded a corner and saw Roy's house ahead. The front porch lights were on, and lights showed through most of the windows. The driveway was packed with cars, most of which Dan recognized as belonging to other Essex residents. What's going on? he wondered. A community meeting? On Halloween?

He parked his truck next to Tom Paulsen's new Cadillac and walked up the front porch steps to the door. As he knocked, a long keening animal cry came from the woods behind Hathaway's house. Bobcat, he thought. The woods are full of 'em.

Laura Hathaway, an attractive gray-haired woman in her mid-fifties, answered the door with a cheerful, "Happy Halloween, Dan!"

"Hi! Happy Halloween." He stepped into the house and could smell the aromatic cherry pipe tobacco Roy favored. The Hathaways had some nice oil paintings on their walls and all their furniture looked new. "What's going on?"

"The men are down in the rumpus room," she explained. "They're having their little yearly get-together." She started to lead him to another door that would take him downstairs. She limped a bit when she walked. Several years ago, Dan understood, a lawnmower had sliced off a few of the toes on her right foot.

"Looks like everybody in Essex is here, with all those cars outside."

She smiled, her kindly face crinkling. "Everybody *is* here, now. Go on down and make yourself at home."

He descended the stairs, and heard Roy's husky voice down there: ". . . Jenny's gold earrings, the ones with the little pearls. Carl, this year it's one of Tiger's new kittens—the one with the black markings on its legs, and that ax you got at the hardware store last week. Phil, he wants one of your piglets and the pickled okra Marcy put in the cupboard . . ."

When Dan reached the bottom of the stairs, Roy stopped talking. The rumpus room, carpeted in bright red because Roy was a Crimson Tide fan, was filled with men from the Essex community. Roy, a hefty man with white hair and friendly, deep-set blue eyes, was sitting in a chair in the midst of them, reading from some kind of list. The others sat around him, listening intently. Roy looked up at Dan, as did the other men, and puffed thoughtfully on his pipe. "Howdy, Dan. Grab yourself a cup of coffee and sit a spell."

"I got your message. What kind of meeting is this?" He glanced around, saw faces he knew: Steve Mallory, Phil Kane, Carl Lansing, Andy McCutcheon, and more. A pot of coffee, cups, and a platter of sandwiches were placed on a table on one side of the room.

"Be with you in a minute," Roy said. While Dan, still puzzled about what was so important on Halloween, poured himself a cup of coffee, he listened to Roy reading from the list he held. "Okay, where were we? Phil, that's it for you, I reckon. Next is Tom. This year it's that ship model you put together, a pair of Ann's shoes—the gray ones she bought in Birmingham—and Tom Junior's G.I. Joe doll. Andy, he wants . . ."

Huh? Dan thought as he sipped at the hot black coffee. He looked at Tom, who seemed to have released a breath he'd been holding for a long time. Tom's model of *Old Ironsides* had taken him months to put together, Dan knew. Dan's gaze snagged other eyes that quickly looked away. He noted that Mitch Brantley, whose wife had just had their first child in July, looked ill; Mitch's face was the color of wet cotton. A haze of smoke hung in the air from Roy's pipe and several other smokers' cigarettes. Cups rattled against saucers. Dan looked at Aaron Greene, who stared back at him through strange, glassy eyes. Aaron's wife, Dan had heard, had died of a heart attack last year about this time. Aaron had shown him pictures of her, a robust-looking brunette in her late thirties.

". . . your golf clubs, your silver cuff links, and Tweetybird," Roy continued.

Andy McCutcheon laughed nervously. In his pallid, fleshy face his eyes were dark and troubled. "Roy, my little girl loves that canary. I mean . . . she's real attached to it."

Roy smiled. It was a tight, false smile, and something about it started a knot of tension growing in Dan's stomach. "You can buy her another one, Andy," he said. "Can't you?"

"Sure, but she loves—"

"One canary's just like another." He drew at his pipe, and when he lifted a hand to hold the bowl the overhead light glinted off the large diamond ring he wore.

"Excuse me, gents." Dan stepped forward. "I sure would like for somebody to tell me what this is all about. My wife and little girl are getting ready for Halloween."

"So are we," Roy replied, and blew out a plume of smoke. "So are we." He traced his finger down the list. Dan saw that the paper was mottled and dirty; it looked as if it had been used to wipe out the inside of a garbage can. The writing on it was scrawled and spiky. "Dan," Roy said, and tapped the paper. "This year he wants two things from you. First is a set of fingernail clippings. Your own fingernails. The second is—"

"Hold on." Dan tried to smile, but couldn't. "I don't get this. How about starting from the beginning."

Roy stared at him for a long, silent moment. Dan felt other eyes on him, watching him carefully. On the opposite side of the room, Walter Ferguson suddenly began quietly sobbing. "Oh," Roy said. "Sure. It's your first Halloween in Essex, isn't it?"

"Right. And?"

"Sit down, Dan." Roy motioned toward an empty chair near him. "Come on, sit down and I'll tell you."

Dan didn't like the feeling in this room; there was too much tension and fear in here. Walter's sobbing was louder. "Tom," Roy said, "take Walter out for a breath of air, won't you?" Tom muttered an assent and helped the crying man out of his chair. When they had left the rumpus room, Roy struck a kitchen match to relight his pipe and looked calmly at Dan Burgess.

"So tell me," Dan urged as he sat down. He did smile this time, but the smile would not stick.

"It's Halloween," Roy explained, as if speaking to a retarded child. "We're going over the Halloween list."

Dan laughed involuntarily. "Is this a joke, gents? What kind of Halloween list?"

Roy's thick white brows came together as he gathered his thoughts. Dan realized the other man was wearing the same dark red sweater he'd worn the day Dan had signed that lease and cut his finger. "Call it . . . a trick-or-treat list, Dan. You know, we all like you. You're a good man. We can't think of a better neighbor to have in Essex." He glanced around as some of the others nodded. "Essex is a very special place to live, Dan. You must know that by now."

"Sure. It's great. Karen and I love it here."

"We all do. Some of us have lived here for a long time. We appreciate the good life we have here. And in Essex, Dan, Halloween is a very special night of the year."

Dan frowned. "I'm not following you."

Roy produced a gold pocket watch, popped it open to look at the time, then closed it again. When he lifted his gaze, his eyes seemed darker and more powerful than Dan had ever seen them. They made him shiver to his soul. "Do you believe in the Devil?" Roy asked.

Again, Dan laughed. "What are we doing, telling spooky stories?" He looked around the room. No one else was laughing.

"When you came to Essex," Roy said softly, "you were a loser. Down on your luck. No job. Your money was almost gone. Your credit rating was zero. You had an old car that was ready for the junkyard. Now I want you to think back on all the good things that have happened to you—all the things you might have taken as a run of good luck—since you've been part of our community. You've gotten everything you've wanted, haven't you? Money's come to you like never before. You got yourself a brand new truck. A promotion at the plant. And there'll be more good things to come in the years ahead—if you cooperate."

"Cooperate?" He didn't like the sound of that word. "Cooperate how?"

"With the list. Like we all do, every Halloween. Every October thirty-first I find a list just like this one, under the welcome mat at the front door. Why I've been chosen to handle it, I don't know. Maybe because I help bring new people in. These items on this list are to be left in front of your door on Halloween. In the morning, they're gone. He comes during the night, Dan, and he takes them away with him."

"This is a Halloween joke, isn't it!" Dan grinned. "Jesus Christ, you gents had me going! That's a hell of an act to put on just to scare the crap out of *me!*"

But Roy's face remained impassive. Smoke seeped from a corner of his wrinkled mouth. "The things," Roy continued evenly, "have to be collected and left out before midnight, Dan. If you don't collect the items and leave them for him, he'll come knocking at your door. And you don't want that, Dan. You really don't."

A chunk of ice seemed to have jammed itself in Dan's throat, while the rest of his body felt feverish. The Devil in Essex? Collecting things like golf clubs and cuff links, ship models and pet canaries? "You're crazy!" he managed to say. "If this isn't a damned joke, you've dropped both your oars into the water!"

"It's no joke, and he ain't crazy," Phil Kane said, sitting behind Roy. Phil was a large, humorless man who raised pigs on a farm about a mile away. "It's just once a year. Just on Halloween. Hell, last year alone I won one of them magazine sweepstakes. It was fifteen thousand dollars at one whack! The year before that, an uncle I didn't even know I had died and left me a hundred acres of land in California. We get free stuff in the mail all the time. It's just once a year we have to give him what *he* wants."

"Laura and I go to art auctions in Birmingham," Roy said. "We always get what we want for the lowest bid. And the paintings are always worth five or ten times what we pay. Last Halloween he asked for a lock of Laura's hair and one of my old shirts with blood on it where I cut myself shaving. You remember that trip to Bermuda the real estate company gave us last summer? I've been given a huge expense account too, and no matter what I charge, nobody asks any questions. He gives us everything we want."

Trick-or-treat! Dan thought crazily. He envisioned some hulking, monstrous form lugging off a set of golf clubs, one of Phil's piglets, and Tom's *Old Ironsides.* God, it was insane! Did these men really believe they were making sacrifices to a satanic trick-or-treater?

Roy lifted his eyebrows. "You didn't return the shotgun, did you? Nor the money. You didn't refuse the promotion."

"I *earned* that promotion!" Dan insisted, but his voice was strained and weak, and it shamed him.

"You signed the agreement in blood," Roy said, and Dan remembered the drops of blood falling from his cut finger onto the white paper of the lease, right underneath his name. "Whether you knew it or not, you agreed to something that's been going on in Essex for over a hundred years. You can have anything and everything you want, Dan, if you give him what *he* wants on one special night of the year."

"My God," Dan whispered. He felt dizzy and sick. If it *was* true . . . what had he stumbled into? "You said . . . he wants two things from me. The fingernail clippings and what else?"

Roy looked at the list and cleared his throat. "He wants the clippings, and . . . he wants the first joint of the little finger of your child's left hand."

Dan sat motionless. He stared straight ahead and feared for an awful moment that he would start laughing and giggle himself all the way to an asylum.

"It's really not much," Roy said. "There won't be a lot of blood, will there, Carl?"

Carl Lansing, who worked as a butcher at the Food Giant in Barrimore Crossing, raised his left hand to show Dan Burgess. "Not much pain if you do it quick, with a cleaver. One sharp blow'll snap the bone. She won't feel a whole lot of pain if you do it fast."

Dan swallowed. Carl's slicked-back black hair gleamed with Vitalis under the light. Dan had always wondered exactly how Carl had lost the thumb of his left hand.

"If you don't put what he wants in front of your door," Andy McCutcheon said, "he'll come in after it. And then he'll take more than he asked for in the first place, Dan. God help you if he has to knock at your door."

Dan's eyes felt like frozen stones in his rigid face; he stared across the room at Mitch Brantley, who appeared to be about to either faint or throw up. Dan thought of Mitch's new son, and he did not want to think about what might be on the list beside either Mitch's or Walter Ferguson's name. He rose unsteadily from his chair. It was not that he believed the Devil was coming to his house tonight for a bizarre trick-or-treat that frightened him so deeply; it was that he knew *they* believed, and he didn't know how to deal with it.

"Dan," Roy Hathaway said gently, "we're all in this together. It's not so bad. Really it isn't. Usually all he wants are little things. Things that don't matter very much." Mitch made a soft, strangled groaning sound. Dan flinched, but Roy paid no attention. Dan had the sudden urge to leap at Roy and grab him by the front of that blood-red sweater and shake him until he split open. "Once in a while he . . . takes something of value," Roy said, "but not very often. And he always gives us back so much more than he takes."

"You're crazy. All of you . . . are crazy."

"Give him what he wants." Steve Mallory spoke in the strong bass voice that was so distinctive in the Baptist church choir on

Sunday mornings. "Do it, Dan. Don't make him knock at your door."

"Do it," Roy told him. "For your own sake, and for your family's."

Dan backed away from them. Then he turned and ran up the stairs, ran out of the house as Laura Hathaway was coming out of the kitchen with a big bowl of pretzels, ran down the front steps and across the lawn to his pickup. Near Steve Mallory's new silver Chevy, Walter and Tom were standing together. Dan heard Walter sob, ". . . not her *ear,* Tom! Dear God, not her whole *ear!*"

Dan got into his truck and left twin streaks of rubber on the pavement as he drove away.

Dead leaves whirled through the chilly air as Dan pulled up into his driveway, got out, and ran up the front porch steps. Karen had taped a cardboard skeleton to the door. His heart was pounding, and he'd decided to take no chances; if this was an elaborate joke, they could laugh their asses off at him, but he was getting Karen and Jaime out of here.

Halfway home, a thought had occurred to him that had almost made him pull off the road to puke: if the list had demanded a lock of Jaime's hair, would he have given it without question? How about her fingernail clippings? A whole fingernail? An earlobe? And if he had given any of those things, what would be on the trick-or-treat list next year and the year after that?

Not much blood, if you do it quick.

"Karen!" he shouted as he unlocked the door and went in. The house was too quiet. *"Karen!"*

"Lord, Dan! What are you yelling about?" She came into the front room from the hallway, followed by Jaime in clown makeup, an oversized red blouse, patched little blue jeans, and sneakers covered with round yellow happy-face stickers. Dan knew he must look like walking death, because Karen stopped as if she'd run into a wall when she saw him. "What's happened?" she asked fearfully.

"Listen to me. Don't ask any questions." He wiped the sheen of sweat off his forehead with a trembling hand. Jaime's soft brown eyes reflected the terror he'd brought into the house with him. "We're leaving right now. We're going to drive to Birmingham and check into a motel."

"It's Halloween!" Karen said. "We might have some trick-or-treaters!"

"Please . . . don't argue with me! We've got to get out of here right now!" Dan jerked his gaze away from his child's left hand; he'd been looking at her little finger and thinking terrible thoughts. "Right now," he repeated.

Jaime was stunned, about to cry. On a table beside her was a plate with the Halloween candies on it—grinning pumpkins with silver eyes and licorice mouths. "We have to go," Dan said hoarsely. "I can't tell you why, but we have to." Before Karen could say anything else, Dan told her to gather whatever she wanted—toothpaste, a jacket, underwear—while he went out and started the truck. But *hurry!* he urged her. For God's sake, hurry!

Outside, dead leaves snapped at his cheeks and sailed past his head. He slid behind the pickup's wheel, put the key into the ignition, and turned it.

The engine made one long groaning noise, rattled, and died.

Christ! Dan thought, close to panic. He'd never had any problem with the truck before! He pumped the accelerator and tried again. The engine was stone cold dead, and all the warning lights—brake fluid, engine oil, battery, even gasoline—flashed red on the instrument panel.

Of course, he realized. Of course. He had paid off the truck with the money he'd won. The truck had been given to him while he was a resident of Essex—and now whatever was coming to their house tonight didn't want him driving that truck *away* from Essex.

They could run for it. Run along the road. But what if they ran into the Halloween visitor, there in the lonely darkness? What if it came up behind them on the road, demanding its trick-or-treat like a particularly nasty child?

He tried the truck again. Dead.

Inside the house, Dan slammed the door and locked it. He went to the kitchen door and locked that too, his wife and daughter watching him as if he'd lost his mind. Dan shouted, "Karen, check all the windows! Make sure they're shut tight! Hurry, damn it!" He went to the closet and took out his shotgun, got a box of shells off the shelf; he opened the box, put it on the table next to the pumpkin candies, broke open the gun's breech, and stuffed two shells into the chambers. Then he closed the breech and looked up as Karen and Jaime returned, clinging to each other.

"All . . . the windows are shut," Karen whispered, her scared blue eyes flickering back and forth from Dan's face to the shotgun. "Dan, what's wrong with you?"

"Something's coming to our door tonight," he replied. "Something terrible. We're going to have to hold it off. I don't know if we can, but we have to try. Do you understand what I'm saying?"

"It's . . . Halloween," she said, and he saw she thought he was totally cracked.

The telephone! he thought suddenly, and ran for it. He picked up the receiver and dialed for the operator in Barrimore Crossing to call for a police car. *Officer, the Devil's on his way to our house tonight and we don't have his favorite kind of candy.*

But on the other end of the line was a piercing crackle of static that sounded like a peal of eerie laughter. Through the static Dan heard things that made him believe he'd truly hurtled over the edge: the crazy theme music from a Porky Pig cartoon, a crash of cymbals, the military drumming of a marching band, assorted gurgles and gasps and moans as if he'd been plugged into a graveyard party line. Dan dropped the receiver, and it dangled from its cord like a lynched corpse. Have to think, he told himself. Figure things out. Hold the bastard off. Got to hold him off. He looked at the fireplace and felt a new hammerblow of horror. "Dear God!" he shouted. "We've got to block up the chimney!"

Dan got on his knees, reached up the chimney, and closed the flue. There were already pine logs, kindling, and newspapers in the fireplace, ready for the first cold night of the year. He went into the kitchen, got a box of Red Top matches, and put them into the breast pocket of his shirt; when he came back into the room, Jaime was crying and Karen was holding her tightly, whispering, "Shhhhh, darling. Shhhhhh." She watched her husband the way one would watch a dog with foam on its mouth.

Dan pulled a chair about ten feet from the front door and sat down with the shotgun across his knees. His eyes were sunken into his head and ringed with purple. He looked at his new Bulova watch; somehow, the crystal had shattered and the hands had snapped off.

"Dan," Karen said—and then she too started to cry.

"I love you, honey," he told her. "You know I love both of you, don't you? I swear I do. I won't let him in. I won't give him what he wants. Because if I do that, what will he take next year? I love you both, and I want you to remember that."

"Oh God . . . Dan . . ."

"They think I'm going to do it and leave it outside the door for him," Dan said. His hands were gripped tightly around the shotgun, his knuckles white. "They think I could take a cleaver and—"

The lights flickered, and Karen screamed. Jaime's wail joined hers.

Dan felt his face contorting with fear. The lights flickered, flickered—and went out.

"He's coming," Dan rasped. "He's coming soon." He stood up, walked to the fireplace, bent down, and struck a match. It took four matches to get the fire going right; its orange light turned the room into a Halloween chamber of horrors, and smoke repelled from the blocked flue swept around the walls like searching spirits. Karen was pressed against the wall, and Jaime's clown makeup was streaming down her cheeks.

Dan returned to the chair, his eyes stinging with smoke, and watched the door.

He didn't know how much longer it was when he sensed something on the front porch. Smoke was filling the house, but the room had suddenly become bone-achingly cold. He thought he heard something scratching out there on the porch, searching around the door for the items that weren't there.

He'll come knocking at your door. And you don't want that. You really don't.

"Dan—"

"Shhhh," he warned her. "Listen! He's out there."

"Him? *Who?* I don't hear—"

There was a knock at the door like a sledgehammer striking the wood. Dan saw the door tremble through the smoke-haze. The knock was followed by a second, with more force. Then a third that made the door bend inward like cardboard.

"Go away!" Dan shouted. "There's nothing for you here!"

Silence.

It's all a trick! he thought. Roy and Tom and Carl and Steve and all the rest are out there in the dark, laughing fit to bust a gut!

But the room was getting viciously cold. Dan shivered, saw his breath float away past his face.

Something scraped on the roof above their heads, like claws seeking a weak chink in the shingles.

"GO AWAY!" Dan's voice cracked. "GO AWAY, YOU BASTARD!"

The scraping stopped. After a long moment of silence, something smashed against the roof like an anvil being dropped. The entire house groaned. Jaime screamed, and Karen shouted, "What is it, Dan, what is it out there?"

Immediately following was a chorus of laughter from beyond the front door. Someone said, "Okay, I guess that's enough!" A different voice called, "Hey, Dan! You can open up now! Just kiddin'!" A third voice said, "Trick-or-treat, Danny boy!"

He recognized Carl Lansing's voice. There was more laughter, more whooping cries of "Trick-or-treat!"

My God! Dan rose to his feet. It's a joke. A brutal, ridiculous joke!

"Open the door!" Carl called. "We can't wait to see your face!"

Dan almost cried, but there was rage building in him and he thought he might just aim the shotgun at them and threaten to shoot their balls off. Were they all crazy? How had they managed the phone and the lights? Was this some kind of insane initiation to Essex? He went to the door on shaky legs, unlocked it—

Behind him, Karen said suddenly, "Dan, *don't!*"

—and opened the door.

Carl Lansing stood on the porch. His black hair was slicked back, his eyes as bright as new pennies. He looked like the cat that had swallowed the canary.

"You damned fools!" Dan raged. "Do you know what kind of scare you people put into me and my family? I ought to shoot your damned—"

And then he stopped, because he realized Carl was standing alone on the porch.

Carl grinned. His teeth were black. "Trick-or-treat," he whispered, and raised the ax that he'd been holding behind his back.

With a cry of terror, Dan stumbled backward and raised the shotgun. The thing that had assumed Carl's shape oozed across the threshold, orange firelight glinting off the upraised ax blade.

Dan squeezed the shotgun's trigger, but the gun didn't go off. Neither barrel would fire. Jammed! he thought wildly, and broke open the breech to clear it.

There were no shells in the shotgun. Jammed into the chambers were Karen's pumpkin candies.

"TRICK-OR-TREAT, DAN!" the thing wailed. "TRICK-OR-TREAT!"

Dan struck into the Carl-thing's stomach with the butt of the shotgun. From its mouth sprayed a mess of yellow canary feathers, pieces of a kitten and what might have been a piglet. Dan hit it again, and the entire body collapsed like an exploding gasbag. Then he grabbed Karen's hand in a frantic blur of motion and was pulling her with him out the door. She held on to Jaime, and they ran down the porch steps and across the grass, along the driveway and the road and toward the main highway with the Halloween wind clutching around them.

Dan looked back, saw nothing but darkness. Jaime shrieked in tune with the wind. The distant lights of other Essex houses glinted in the hills like cold stars.

They reached the highway. Dan shouldered Jaime, and still they ran into the night, along the roadside where the high weeds caught at their ankles.

"Look!" Karen cried out. "Somebody's coming, Dan! Look!"

Headlights were approaching. Dan stood in the middle of the road, frantically waving. The vehicle—a gray Volkswagen van—began to slow down. At the wheel was a woman in a witch costume, and next to her two children dressed like ghosts peered out the window. People from Barrimore Crossing! Dan realized. Thank God! "Help us!" he begged. "Please! We've got to get out of here!"

"You in trouble?" the woman asked. "You have an accident or something?"

"Yes! An accident! Please, get us to the police station in Barrimore Crossing! I'll pay you! Just please get us there!"

The woman paused. Then she said, "Okay. Climb in." Dan pulled open the van's side door.

They started off, the engine backfiring, toward Barrimore Crossing.

"I don't see no accident," the woman said. "You have a car wreck or what?"

Dan shook his head. The two ghost-children were watching him over the front seat. In his arms, Jaime was dazed and shaking.

"We're okay," he managed to say to Karen, and took her hand. "We're safe now, honey."

And something wet dripped onto his cheek.

He looked up at the van's ceiling.

The van had teeth.

Long rows of triangular, serrated teeth.

As his mind cracked and he began to laugh, he saw the sticky fluid dripping down off the teeth, saw in the green glow of the instrument panel more teeth pushing up from the van's soft, wet gray sides and floorboard.

His last coherent thought, as Karen's scream filled his head, was that the Devil sure could come up with one hell of a costume.

"Trick-or-treat, Dan," the shape at the wheel said.

And the entire van smashed shut like a huge mouth, the teeth grinding down until bone and flesh were pulverized and unrecognizable.

Then the van, looking more like a large shiny roach, scuttled off the road toward the Essex woods. It changed shape into something that would drive a man mad to behold—and then it was gone into the hills, with its bellyful of Halloween treats.

Introduction:

Eyes

BY CHARLES L. GRANT

Charles L. Grant is one of the best-known American writers and anthologists in the field of horror. His novels include the Oxrun Station series, *The Nestling, Night Songs,* and *The Tea Party.* But he is best known for his hauntingly dark short stories, collected in *Tales from the Night-Side, A Glow of Unicorns,* and *Nightmare Seasons.*

Grant is a proponent of what he calls "quiet" horror: subtle, dark, with a lingering bitter aftertaste. For this book, I urged him to write something nasty. Something *really* nasty. The result is "Eyes."

Eyes

BY CHARLES L. GRANT

The leaves were gone when the wind returned past sunset, and there was nothing left to do but help the empty branches claw at the sky. An unlatched gate fought its brown-rusted hinges. An empty silver trash can toppled off the curb, its lid a clattering pinwheel until it struck the rear bumper of a small truck at the corner. A shutter banged open, slammed shut, and froze. Curtains trembled. Shadows walked. Streetlamps grew brittle, hazed white light without a promise of warmth. The only traffic signal in town swayed like a hanged man, tugging at its guy wires until it flared just red.

And the leaves on the ground, here raked into piles and there untouched and turning brown, hunched and spun madly into man-high dervishes that slammed against hedges, exploded against porches, crested off sidewalks into the windshields of passing cars. They hissed and crackled, their edges age-sharp and stinging, and when they swept past lighted windows they were hunting bats enraged.

Ron turned his back against the leaf-woven wind and waited for the gust to pass him by. The collar of his black trench coat was snapped up in back and folded out in front, the gold-buckled belt cinched tight around his waist. All he needed, he thought, was the hat Bogart wore, and someone would surely ask him how to get to Casablanca. As it was, the length of his brown hair tangled around his ears, poked needles at his eyes, and there was no sense brushing it back because the wind was still there.

He didn't mind it. Standing out here, in the cold, in the dark, made him feel as if he were stalking a killer, or a spy, or a warlock determined to conquer the world with mad spells. It certainly made for better copy than saying he was just waiting for his son.

He grinned to himself. He walked a few paces to the corner and leaned back against the rear fender of a red pickup. In the gutter was the dented metal lid of a trash can, and he almost picked it up before he shrugged and changed his mind.

A gust made him squint, a cat's scream made him jump.

C'mon, Paulie, he urged, it's getting cold out here.

The houses that surrounded him were well lighted and old, comforting in their size and the people who lived there. And it was curious, he thought, how tomorrow they would be transformed into birthplaces of goblins. Of witches. Of burnt-cork hobos out foraging for a candy meal. Even now, as he looked around, he could see the holiday trimmings: stalks of maize taped to the storm doors, cardboard cutouts of ghosts on the windows, a basket of polished apples, black cats hissing.

And the eyes.

As he pushed away from the truck and paced up the street, he could see the eyes watching. Orange eyes, flickering eyes, winking in the wind. Jack-o'-lanterns balanced on porch railings and perched on front stoops, hiding from the cold in the split of a curtain, staring out from a child's bedroom on the second floor, behind the trees. He didn't mind the black cats and the hags and the monsters; he didn't mind the treat-or-treating or the UNICEF brigades; and he didn't even mind the cold jagged grins the pumpkins gave him as he passed. Knowing grins. Dead grins. He didn't mind them much at all.

The eyes, on the other hand, gave him the creeps.

They were up there looking out, looking down, and they saw him.

Paulie knew.

Two years ago Ron was holding his son's hand, and they walked through an Indian summer night to fill the paper bag with candy. They passed several of the boy's schoolmates, all of them greeting him with muffled laughter, with jeers behind his back. Paulie didn't care as long as his father held his hand. And Ron didn't care as long as Paulie knew that some people were cruel when faced with something different, something they were too young, or too secure, or too stupid, to understand.

It happened every year, each Halloween since Paulie had been old enough to get into his costume and walk with him door to door.

But five years ago, when Paulie was nearing ten, a group of

teenagers laughing their way from one house to another began following them, making rude comments until Ron could take no more. He'd turned and faced them, his hands in fists, out where the kids could see them.

"Very brave," he'd said, and the laughter faded as the teenagers huddled, one girl carefully studying the sky. "Very brave."

"Ah, c'mon, Mr. Ritter, we were only kidding."

"No," he'd said, "don't tell me, tell my son."

Paulie had tugged at his hand, wanting to leave, clearly afraid.

"No, you tell my son you think he's funny. Go ahead, tell him to his face."

They muttered, shuffled feet, finally turned and walked away. None of them looked back, and Ron filled his lungs with the warm night air.

"Daddy?"

"It's okay, pal, it's okay."

At the corner a boy suddenly whipped around and lifted his middle finger, and Ron reacted before his mind caught up—he broke into a sprint, dropping the paper bag on the sidewalk as the sprint became a charge. The boy gaped, and turned too late. Ron grabbed his shoulders and shoved him hard into a hedge, grabbed his denim jacket in one hand, pulled him close and smiled.

The eyes widened in fear.

Ron slammed a fist into his stomach and shoved him back again. When the boy doubled over, Ron put a knee to his chin and stepped back to avoid the blood from the split lip and the slashed gums. Then he glared at the rest of them, some ready to run, two ready to fight.

"Go ahead," he invited, still smiling. "Go ahead. And when you're done with me you can beat up on the retard."

One of them, a girl, caught a gasp behind a palm.

"Hey," Ron said, "that's what you're thinking, right? The kid's a retard. He looks funny, walks funny, maybe dribbles a little when he tries to talk. A clown, right? No problem. He can't hurt you."

"Mister, that isn't fair."

He nodded. "You're right, little girl. It isn't fair at all, but you don't have the slightest idea what I'm talking about. Not the slightest idea in hell." Then he'd spun around and hooked the fallen boy by the collar, yanked him to his feet, and virtually thrown him at his friends. "Clean him up," he ordered in disgust. "Clean the bastard up; he's a disgrace to this town."

As he returned to his son, poor Paulie standing all alone in the middle of the sidewalk, holding the paper bag his father had dropped, his Batman's cape limp, his store-bought costume not quite fitting, Ron began to cry. He was glad he'd hit the kid; for years he'd wanted to do something like that and every time the urge took shape every convention in the book had stopped him, had held him; he'd long since stopped telling Irma because she thought it was childish. Hell, maybe it was, but it sure felt great. In the morning he'd probably get a call from the police, and his wife would shake her head sadly and wonder why he didn't stop and *think.* But he felt good, and there was no way at all he could explain that to Paulie.

"Wrong, Daddy," the boy had said then, surprising Ron to a halt. He looked down at the blue eyes, innocent, almost blank, and saw the disappointment. "Wrong, Daddy, wrong."

Over and over for the rest of the night until he'd finally lost his temper and dragged the boy home, refusing him any of his candy until the next day. But it was less at his son than at himself that his anger had flared—by hitting that punk he had contradicted everything he'd tried to teach Paulie from the time he could understand.

The following year he bought the pumpkin.

A dog chained in a backyard began howling and barking. Leaves caught in a storm drain stirred and rustled under the wind. A large dead beetle lay in the middle of the sidewalk, and his heel crunched the hard shell before he could avoid it. The temperature dropped, and his breath began to fog. The gutters were black with shadows. A woman laughed. The stars waited. The slow-dying grass began to grey with early frost.

And the eyes.

The houses went dark, but the candles were still burning, and the eyes brightened and dimmed and watched him pass through the black, dressed in black, avoiding their looks from over there on the rocker, and over there on the mat, and over there on the brick house at the corner where they gathered on the roof like the angry souls of waiting cats.

He shuddered, and watched his feet stepping over the cracks

and around shadow-puddles that weren't puddles at all. An empty pack of cigarettes was kicked to one side. A bottle cap squashed flat looked too much like a penny. He adjusted his collar more snugly around his neck and slipped his hands into his pockets, pursing his lips to try a silent whistle, failing, and grinning self-consciously as if someone had seen him.

The street rose slightly and the houses began to drift apart, longer stretches between yards, higher screens of dark shrubs. By the time he reached the top he was beginning to breathe heavily, and scolded himself for smoking too much when he knew what was coming, when he knew he'd need the wind. Another grin, this one mocking—wind, stamina, strong legs, what the hell. Paulie wouldn't care.

The trouble had been the pumpkin.

He'd come home that year with the great thing in his arms, his cheeks puffed with exertion as he staggered into the kitchen and thumped it on the table. Irma was settled in the front room, knitting, scowling, telling him with her eyes that the boy didn't know what was going on and she thought he was being silly, perhaps even cruel. But Paulie had danced, a clumsy shuffle on the tiled floor that made Ron smile a little sadly. Then he spread out the newspapers, brought out the knife and ladle, and with a running commentary spiked with bad jokes, he hollowed out the pumpkin. He tried not to seem nervous, but this was the first time he'd ever done it and he wanted Paulie to believe his father knew it all.

Paulie sat in his chair, chin in his hands, eyes on the knife and the ladle and the seeds on the paper. A faint line of saliva glinted on his chin. He was pale.

With a felt-tip pen Ron drew the gap-toothed mouth, the triangle nose, and with his tongue between his lips, tried to make the eyes straight. He knew they had to be triangular as well, but somehow they wouldn't work, and when he felt his patience going he shrugged to Paulie and decided to start in by carving the mouth first.

Paulie wanted to help.

Ron denied him gently.

Paulie pouted and frowned, shaking the table to unsteady his hand.

At the nose, the knife slipped and cut Ron slightly on the thumb.

Paulie's eyes widened in fascination and fright, but his father didn't yell, didn't shout. He gnawed his lower lip and took up the knife again. A smile to show that everything was fine, don't worry, I'll live, and he carved the first eye—slowly, grunting to himself, finally shoving the thick piece free into the pumpkin. A grin of satisfaction, and the second one was done.

"Try, Daddy?"

He shook his head. "Son, you know better. This knife is too sharp. Besides, I'm already finished."

"Try!"

"Paulie, no. A pumpkin's like a person, it has only two eyes."

Paulie scowled, then lunged across the table to snatch the knife away and began stabbing at the pumpkin's finished face. Ron grabbed his wrist and squeezed until the boy whimpered, squeezed until the knife clattered to the floor.

The pumpkin fell from the table, hit its side, and shattered.

"Try," Paulie sobbed, wiping his face with the backs of his hands.

"Two eyes, you stupid brat! You only get two goddamned eyes!"

"Wrong, Daddy."

He felt like crying himself, suddenly threw his arms around the boy and hugged him, rocked him, told him he was sorry but there were things going on, in the house and at work, that he'd never understand. He didn't mean to take it out on the one person who couldn't fight back.

"Wrong, Daddy, wrong."

Then Paulie had plunged his hands into the wreckage and pulled out the triangle wedges poked from the eyes. He stood and held them to his face, grinned, and marched away. Ron lunged for him, and succeeded only in giving him a slight shove through the doorway. Blinded by the pumpkin shards, Paulie tripped over the loose edge of the rug and struck his head on the dining room table. There wasn't much blood. There didn't have to be blood.

The corner had gone straight into his eye.

Just beyond the top of the street rise, the church reached out of the dark ground, a black silhouette cut from the sky in spite of the moon. It was small, steepled, set back from the sidewalk behind a low picket fence. There was no parking lot; parishioners used the streets and walked up the flagstone path to the dark oak double doors. On either side, maple and elm loomed as high as the belfry; in the back was the graveyard.

Ron stopped at the far corner of the fence and looked around, checking for cars, checking for snoops. All he saw, however, at the bottom of the rise were the yellow flecks blinking furiously as the wind moved the branches, the yellow eyes watching him though they faced the other way. He was alone. He stared past the church to the fieldstone wall, the chained iron gate, the headstones and mausoleums and spread-winged angels that marked the homes of the dead. He couldn't see Paulie's grave from here, but that didn't matter. He visited it once a month, could find it blind if he had to, and he apologized to his son for not giving him longer life, for not having the money for the doctors who might have saved him.

The blunt wedge of pumpkin had been driven almost to his brain.

Well, tomorrow's the big day, he said heartily, silently, rolling his shoulders to drive off the cold. He hoped that Paulie couldn't sense his resignation; what would you like to be this year, son? Space things are pretty big, robots and spacemen and stuff like that.

Orange eyes.

No clouds this year, just lots and lots of stars. I don't think it'll rain like it did last time. Of course, the leaves have all fallen, but you can't have everything, right, Paulie? Right?

Orange eyes in the graveyard.

Maybe good old Batman again, what do you say? I still have all the things in your bedroom. I could iron the cape a little, wash the rest of it and throw it in the dryer before I go to bed, and since you'd have to wear a sweater, it's so cold, you'd look like you had more muscles than anybody in town.

Orange eyes, moving.

Well, you let me know, okay, son? Let me know. I'll be waiting.

His cheeks puffed, and he blew white into the black, sniffed once, and turned back down the hill. The town below was silent. The wind had died. The moon was gone behind a cloud that drove back the stars.

His heels were loud now on the pavement, and the brush of his trench coat against his legs annoyed him. He was cold; he'd done his duty, and he was cold. He'd gone to his son as he promised he would when the boy lay dying in his arms, and he had told him what it would be like on Halloween this year. Four years in a row, and he wondered how long he'd have to keep this up before his nightmares left him.

Paulie writhing and screaming on the dining room floor, his hands clamped against his eye, and the slow red trickle of blood between his fingers. Paulie gulping for air as the ambulance took him. Paulie trying to speak as he was wheeled into surgery.

Paulie dying. Paulie dead.

Irma had left him two weeks later, sobbing that she wanted no part of a man who killed his children.

He reached the first house and paused to wipe a hand across his brow. He closed his eyes for a moment, then looked back over his shoulder.

Orange eyes, moving.

There was a pumpkin in the middle of the sidewalk.

There was a pumpkin squatting in the middle of the road.

All right, Paulie, he thought, stop fooling around.

He moved more quickly, the incline giving him speed and making him colder as the night parted and let him through, let him pass by the eyes in the windows, on the porches, on the roofs, by the eyes glittering and flickering and winking on the lawns, and in the street, and on the pavement behind him.

No shadows; no shadows at all.

I didn't mean it, Paulie, he thought; I was just kidding.

His house had no porch, only a concrete stoop. The pumpkin he kept there had never had a candle, never had a flashlight. The way kids were these days, he knew he'd be lucky if it lasted through the holiday before somebody smashed it. He opened the door and looked behind him. At the eyes. In the yard.

Paulie, damn it!

He closed the door and leaned against it, unbuckling the belt and pulling off his coat. It fell, and he didn't touch it. He stumbled wearily down the hall and into the kitchen, sat at the table and stared at the kettle on the stove. A pumpkin seed lay on the floor by his shoe. He nudged it aside, then cracked his knuckles, rubbed his face, and took a deep breath until he thought he was calm.

Then he focused on the newspaper spread open before him and suddenly decided he'd go to a movie.

He smiled.

A movie. God, it had been months since he'd been in an honest-to-god theater, had popcorn and soda, and stayed for the second show; years since he'd done anything he hadn't done with Paulie. It might be a good thing; hell, it would be a damned good thing. Of course he would still visit the grave and still go through the ritual, but there was no sense sacrificing the rest of his life by living in the past. No sense at all. So a movie it would be. He reached for the paper, soggy and stained orange, and turned the pages gingerly until he found what he wanted. His finger slipped down the column to check the times and the titles, his lips moving as he read, and the lights went out.

The kitchen was dark.

Except for the eyes.

The eyes in the window, and the eyes in the front room; the eyes on the staircase, and the eyes on the stove.

And the eyes in the shadow that came through the back door, triangular eyes, orange and flickering.

The paper turned to ash and flaked to the table, without a spark, without a sound.

"Paulie."

Wrong, Daddy, wrong.

"Paulie, for god's sake."

Do it, Daddy.

Eyes on the ceiling, eyes on the table.

He thought about telling Paulie to go to hell, sighed, and rose stiffly, still cold and tired. He walked to the doorway and looked back with a sigh.

"Paulie, I'm getting awfully sick of doing this every year."

Daddy, try.

"God*damn,* I said I was sorry."

Every Halloween the same damn thing; every Halloween the screaming, and the bleeding, and the agony until dawn; every year the day in bed until it was over and he had eleven months left to get himself ready again. Every year eleven months to think about running, and knowing he couldn't because Paulie wouldn't let him.

Daddy!

"Paulie," he said, suddenly licking his lips, "Paulie, you *are* going to help me, right? I mean, you're not—"

Try, Daddy. Try.

He took a deep breath, and threw himself at the table, turning his head to catch the corner just right.

Eyes.

Introduction:

The Nixon Mask

BY WHITLEY STRIEBER

Whitley Strieber is the author of *The Wolfen, The Hunger, Black Magic,* and *The Night Church,* and co-author of the international bestsellers, *Warday* and *Nature's End.* He puts me in mind of Philip K. Dick's comment that, just because you're paranoid, that doesn't mean they're not out to get you. Here he provides a portrait of one of our Great American Paranoids, Richard M. Nixon.

Imagine Halloween night at the Nixon White House.

The Nixon Mask

BY WHITLEY STRIEBER

Sometimes in the course of a life a sort of hush falls, as if some vast controlling thing had paused in its work, perhaps sensing a chance to pounce. Then, if one has just the right cast of mind, one can feel it staring, tensing, and beginning to come forth. And one can see, in the dark light of universal truth, that even the most ordinary things have shadows.

Such a hush had fallen on the President. He was waiting for the children of the White House staff to ring the bell of the Private Apartment. He bore a tray of perfectly ordinary Halloween candy in his hands. Now he looked down at the pile of candy bars with new eyes. "Pat, do you think—these bonbons—we could have these—"

"They're fine, Dick. They're called Miniature Baby Ruths, not bonbons. The bonbons are for dignitaries."

The President looked at the doubtful little candies. They looked like the exact opposite of something to eat, there was no getting around it. Why had she unwrapped them? The red and white wrappers had been attractive. He put the tray down on the hall table and touched one, feeling the swollen ridges of the thing, hefting it between thumb and forefinger. "I wonder—you know, we could just—these things . . ."

"Do you understand what's required of you, Dick?"

"Of course. All I have to do is just—when the kids come—oh God, Pat, why am I giving them these things?"

The children of the White House staff had been making their costumes for days. The Nixons would rather not have endured their little Halloween ritual, of course. But they had no choice. The President felt the full tension of the moment. He was sure he'd be more confident if only he didn't have this unsightly candy.

If they were displeased—or worse, thought it an affront—the tremendous effort he and Pat were making to prevent an open attack would be wasted. Unless he kept the staff at bay, no president really had a future. He poked at the pile of brown, knobby candies wishing that Pat would just this once allow him to do things the way he wanted to do them.

"Look, I'll call—I know there's not much time—but money's no problem. We can take care of that. That candy man—you've got him in your blue book—wonderful. He'll make marzipan pumpkins—white chocolate ghosts—money . . . it's . . ."

"You could pay him a million dollars—"

"That's no problem."

"And he still wouldn't be able to make you your marzipan goblins in time. The kids will be here in two minutes."

"I've got to take a—my bladder—"

"Then do it, but make it snappy. We can't keep these particular children waiting, you know. Not these children."

As the President urinated he imagined himself down at Key Biscayne, instead of in this satin prison. He'd be sitting out in back with Bebe and Herb Abplanalp, working on a nice cold Jack Daniel's and water and talking about some lovely subject like money or women or fate. As he finished he dripped "Abplanalp, Abplanalp, Abplanalp," into the pristine White House vitreous. "God help—" he muttered to himself, "I wonder if they are—they don't seem . . . children."

"You have forty seconds," Pat shrilled from the front hall.

What was going to be at that door—a band, perhaps, playing *Night on Bald Mountain* as he distributed the unfortunate-looking candies? As he moved down the hall to the staging area he noticed the awful expression on his wife's face. Her eyes, he realized with sorrow, always looked fearful now.

And with good reason. Good, good reason.

"I want a bourbon," he said. "I can't—these damn things can't be touched—they're—they actually appear to be—it's unfortunate. An unfortunate choice."

"I ordered an assortment. I guess this was all they had."

"That's bizarre. What are they thinking of—we could be in danger here. Who did you order from?"

"The kitchen."

"Pat, Pat, you mustn't trust the kitchen. You just must not. It might be staff-infiltrated, for all we know."

"Jacques is my own chef!"

"Even so—well, I suppose we can—I wonder, though—these things—who was going to get them for dessert? My God, I've got the Queen of England—I'd hate to think—to see Her Majesty forced—"

"Even our chef wouldn't give the Queen candy bars for dessert. Mr. Tubman is coming the next week. Maybe they were for him."

"Well, of course, that's the Lithuanian President, isn't it?"

"Liberian."

"Well, one of those. I suppose—those people—even small things can astound them—that man from New Guinea—remember—ate only the heads—the heads—"

The doorbell rang. Nixon snatched up his tray of candy and positioned himself as per plan, just to Pat's left and three steps behind her. She pulled the door open.

The President's lines ran through his head. As always with a staff encounter, he and Pat had rehearsed very, very carefully. You couldn't just talk to the staff. Something might be taken amiss, and the whole delicate relationship destroyed. Working with the staff was like swimming in the same waters with barracuda. You stayed, because 'cuda usually don't bother people, but you were very, very careful and you showed no gold.

"Ah one, a two, a three," said a voice from the shadows behind the children. An adult controller wearing a sheet.

"Trick-or-treat," cried the children in precise unison.

"Oh, goodness," Pat recited, "what scary ghosts, goblins, pirates, and witches." She sounded sick.

A little child stepped forward. Nixon was at once horrified and fascinated to see a grotesque caricature of his own face, a monstrous and absurd rubber mask. The child wore a dark suit and a "quiet" necktie of the type the President himself favored. He carried a glass of what was probably supposed to represent bourbon in his hand. "What will it be, Mr. President," he recited in a sneering singsong, "treats or—tricks!"

"I say, treats," the President replied, his mind reeling, his face riveted on the terrible mask. What did it mean—and why was it so fascinating? It was so unpleasant that he found himself wanting it.

The strength of his interest shocked him into a dangerous mistake. He departed from the script. "Excuse me, child," he said.

Pat sucked in her breath. "For God's sake," she hissed, "that's not your line!"

There was a rustle of excitement from the crowd of children. Some of them made fists or eager, snatching motions with their long, thin fingers.

He hadn't been able to help himself, and they knew it. He had in effect flashed some gold at the 'cuda. Desperately, he cranked up a smile and pushed ahead, intending to return to his lines. Astonishingly, other words came from his lips. "Child, I'm most interested in your mask. Could I see it?" When he realized what he was saying, he felt a rush of blood, and his heart began to pound. Pat moaned.

"Yes, Mr. President," the little creature said. It began to remove the mask.

"Page two: President leans forward and offers tray to children," Pat said, her voice shuddering.

The child who held the mask was beautiful, his skin pale, his hair blond, freckles neatly dusted across his nose in two parallel rows of six each. His cheeks glittered in the soft light, as if they were made of porcelain.

A thousand forgotten images of the season crowded up in the President's mind. Glowing jack-o'-lanterns and the high, sharp moon; the long rustle of old leaves and the patter of feet in the dark. And masks, the most ancient of human artifacts, masks and the things you could do inside them.

The freedom of masks.

The delicious smell of the rubber.

Looking out through eye sockets not your own.

Old rituals . . . witches flying about the fire . . . reindeer blowing and glaciers groaning . . . firelight . . . eyelight . . . cold stars.

The precious ability to hide.

A mask was a tool. A weapon. The President wanted one. That one.

Pat grabbed her husband's shoulder, digging her fingernails in until it hurt. "You give the candy and you back up six steps so I can close the door! You do not take anything from them, Dick! You *do not!*"

The President's tray wobbled as he removed one hand to snatch the mask.

"Children step forward one by one to get their treats," Pat continued. "President makes personal comment on each costume."

The mask tucked under his arm, the President was now able to return to the script. "What a scary ghost," he said.

"This is the pirate," Pat spat. "They've screwed up the order. They're trying to throw us completely off balance!" There were spots of blood on her hands where she had dug her fingernails into her palms.

The President's mouth was dry. He forced himself to keep to his lines. If they could just reach the end of the script and get the door closed, they would have survived another encounter with the strange and monstrous beings who had for so many generations possessed the White House.

A Cinderella came up next. "Uh-oh, do I have to walk the plank, little pirate," the President said. His hands shook as he dropped one of the candies in her bag. At least they smelled like chocolate, despite their appearance.

"Thank you, sir, but I cannot have this dance, for I must be home by midnight."

As the girl retreated, the President spoke his next line, knowing that it must also be out of order, and therefore offer them a chance to intervene. Perhaps even to do something fatal, like come into the Apartment to find the script and correct it. "Ah, my dear girl, how beautiful you are. May I dance just one dance with you?"

"Rowf! Rowf!" replied the next child, who was dressed not as a Cinderella but as a gorilla.

Maybe if he kept working through the thing, it would come out all right. Maybe the next child would be in the agreed order. "Oh, oh, I must run," the President intoned, "or this hairy monster will eat me up!"

Instead of the hairy monster, who was nowhere to be seen, the President found that he had addressed his lines to a tiny girl in meticulously tailored marine battle fatigues. "I've got to go after the gooks," she said, "so I need candy for energy!"

Feeling Pat's eyes boring into his neck, Nixon continued miserably. "Hairy monster took my candy," he recited. "Oh, here comes a vampire. I had better keep my necktie on tight!"

"My dear President," replied a quite beautiful girl of about twelve, "I am the Good Witch of the North, here to say that we have won. Now that you took the treat, you've got to take the tricks as well. All of them." She raised her face, her gray eyes bright, her lips parted in a half-smile. "Try on the mask, Mr. President."

Pat stifled a shriek.

The President shook his head. The Good Witch of the North laughed, a knowing tinkle, and retreated with a flourish of her tinfoil-covered wand.

The event wound to a miserable close, in complete chaos and three minutes behind schedule. "Well," the President said as Pat slammed the door, "like I always say, when things get tough, the tough get—what? Up? No. Let's see, when things get tough, the tough get—"

"Oh, shut up. We're taking a telephone call from John Dean in less than a minute and you've barely even glanced over the script for your side of the conversation. And throw that damned mask in the garbage!"

Dean was the most dangerous member of the staff, maybe even the leader, if they had such things. If Nixon was going to be destroyed, Dean would be the engineer. Nixon, destroyed. It gave him a curious, breathless thrill . . . waiting in his room for Mother's tread on the creaky board outside, Mother with the long, black paddle in her delicate white hand. Nixon waiting. The President . . . waiting. *Nixon.* The President looked down at the mask, fascinated to see his own features twisted through the clinging, pliant rubber.

The telephone rang. "They never let up! They never stop! You'll have to read cold."

Nixon went into the bedroom. He could smell the rubber of the mask, and it was not an unpleasant smell. As a boy back in Whittier he had loved Halloween. The Night Between the Worlds. The Night of Misrule. Bat wing and mask.

He remembered his feet crunching on dry grass as the moon rode low, and listening to the tremendous murmur of the dead.

Dogs howled, and the Episcopal bells tolled nine times, and the wind hissed in the leaves . . .

He found that he was crying. He sat down and waited for the three buzzes that would mean Pat had finished her initial sparring with Dean, and he could pick up the phone. He glanced over the script she had so carefully prepared for him. The typing blurred through his tears. She was a soldier, his Pat. How she struggled in his behalf, designing each confrontation with the staff right down to the pauses between sentences, leaving nothing to chance, rehearsing everything, and recording every word that was said on an elaborate system of tape machines.

He was shaking badly now. The mask lay on his lap. He couldn't deny that he wanted to put it on, even though the thought made him sick with fear.

The Good Witch of the North . . . so beautiful, so dangerous.

A mask is a door, really, a secret door. He looked down at the dark eyes, the wrinkled, brutal brow, the familiar nose.

They had given him what he wanted most. All through his childhood he had made disguises, mustaches out of old brushes, false eyebrows from bits of tree moss, masks from papier-mâché. Lovely masks, but not so lovely as this.

The three buzzes came. Nixon snatched up the phone and began reading his script. "Hello, John. Himself is just fine. How are you?"

"Fine, Mr. President."

"John, I've got a few things to discuss with you before I put the President on the line."

"You're the President."

"First, I want an explanation of why you fired his personal secretary. He's had Rose Mary with him for years and years. I don't want that plastic girl you've put in her place, Mo, I think she's called. I want you to give him his Rose Mary back."

"Pat just asked me that. And since when did you start talking in complete sentences?"

"He can't work without Rose Mary. I'm just going to have to draw the line. I ordered your girl out this morning and, believe me, she is not coming back."

"Pat just said that. What's going on?"

The First Lady strode into the room and snatched the President's script out of his hands. "Dick, this is your copy of *my* dialogue! Look, can't you read—right here, Mrs. Nixon, 31 October '71, Dean Telephone Call, Schedule 8:11 P.M." She tore the copy to shreds. "That takes care of that! Now read your own script or we'll seem weaker than we already do—if that's possible." The

President fumbled around the top of the bedside table. With a swoop of her hand, Pat produced the correct script. "Here, read!"

"Hiya, John, this is—how are you?"

"I'm fine, sir. How are you?"

"Oh, I just—Halloween with the White House—you know, the cook's and so forth—kids."

"Yeah, that must have been fun. Look, I called to talk over this matter of intelligence. We're just not getting the kind of intelligence we need on the Democrats."

"Oh, that is a problem. Of course, we have—we have sources—sources there."

"Yes, we do. But we'd like to let this Liddy character go in there."

"Ah, well—I wonder—the implications of that are always—what about Mitchell?"

"He's in the boat on this. We need a strike force is what we need. We want to just neutralize those people completely. Go right into their operation in the Watergate and put in some equipment."

"We don't have any problems there, John."

"Then I have your approval to proceed?"

"Ah, well—the job has to be done."

"Thank you, Mr. President." Dean rang off. The President put down the phone and sighed. He was just beginning to push his right shoe off with his left foot when the phone rang again. Pat picked up.

"I'm sorry," she said, "the President is closed except for crisis management until 0900 tomorrow." She put it down.

"Who—"

"Nobody. You're closed after eight, remember. Except to Dean and the staff, of course. And that wasn't one of them."

Here he was, President of the United States, and he couldn't even take a phone call without getting permission from his so-called staff. His whole body ached. He was exhausted.

Pat moved slowly about, getting ready for bed.

The President, watching his poor wife, determined to end her suffering. This resistance to the staff was pointless. Look where resistance had gotten Lincoln and McKinley and Kennedy. And Johnson—he had played along but they just didn't like him. For that matter, they didn't like Dick Nixon much either. But look at the way they fawned when Jerry Ford came around. Him they loved, the poor dumb lunk. They had hated Wilson and poor Cleveland and Grant, and ruined all three. The Roosevelts, though, they had loved, and Ike seemed to have gotten along with them reasonably well.

All those years Ike was in the White House, the Nixons hadn't known a thing about what was really going on. Mamie's condition should have told them something was wrong, though. "Hell looks like heaven," Mamie had said once.

Nixon remembered that day, the four of them together down at Gettysburg. A fine autumn day. What had the discussion been about? Nixon couldn't recall. What he did remember was the click of golf balls, the whine of the cart, the cawing of a crow that kept diving at Ike's bald spot. And Mamie, all in white, drinking Cutty and water and talking in her sad, careful voice.

Pat's voice was also sad and careful.

He raised the mask to his face.

"Oh God, God, Dick no! *No!*"

"Oh, come on, Pat."

"Don't put that on! You'll become—a—one of them!"

Anger flared in him. "If Dwight D. Eisenhower saw fit to play their game, Richard Nixon can damn well play too. We're being arrogant, Patty-girl. And we'll pay if we keep it up. I really don't want to get my brains spattered across the backseat of a damn Lincoln Continental like Jack."

She stared, her eyes bulging in horror. "Don't do that, you'll destroy everything we've built."

"It's a Halloween mask."

"Remember the story of the Poisoned Apple. Remember the Trojan Horse!"

He looked at her dry face, the skin so tight, the lips twisted in terror. As if in slow motion, her quivering fingers came toward him, jutting from her bony hands. "Give me that mask."

"Pat—we can—I really—"

"Give me that—that *thing!*"

He drew back from her.

"Don't you understand even yet what this house is all about, what these people who live in it *are?*"

"I—of course—but you can't fight—there's no way."

"I hate the White House. I wish to God you hadn't wanted it. Oh, Dick, you actually *wanted* it!"

"I—it isn't quite that clear—but of course—"

"You wanted it, Richard Nixon. You wanted to live in this charnel house!"

"I was—you can't know—I promised Ike—"

She slumped, weeping, into a chair. The Lincoln portrait glowered down at her. It hurt his heart to see her as she was. His fine old friend. His protector. He remembered her girlhood, her music.

Slowly she raised her eyes. She looked at him "You—for the love of God—you lost. They got into you all right, didn't they? You're going to put on that mask now because you've no choice." Her voice rose to a stricken howl. "They've won. They own you!"

"I'm going to just—it's actually a little funny, don't you—"

"Funny! Have you taken leave of your senses?"

He felt, on the contrary, that he had come to his senses. He raised the mask. She uttered a broken, defeated sob. "If I put this on, we'll survive, Pat. It's the only way."

"Don't!"

He snapped it down over his head. The rubber pressed against his nose at once, then against his eyes and cheeks and temples. The mask settled eagerly into the structure of his face. A sensation as of ants scuttling beneath his skin made him want to reach up and claw the flesh away. He hadn't realized it would hurt this much. Not this much! He opened his mouth but he couldn't cry out, the mask covered his lips. His head grew hot and sweaty. He could feel Pat outside, grabbing at him, pulling at the rubber, shrieking. He thought, God, I was wrong, it doesn't control, it kills! Kills and takes over. But she'll think it's just control. She'll think I'm still in here and I won't be! Oh God, Pat, please hear me—please—can't . . . talk . . .

He reeled and hammered, his head swelling and aching, quick rivers of pain coming deep into his skull, and with them the avid whispering of the whole staff, a whispering that rose and rose until it filled Richard Milhouse Nixon's brain and mind and soul. Then the speakers looked for the first time through these new eyes, at the tear-streaked old woman on the outside, and said:

"There now—ha ha—it's just—you see—a mask after all. Just—a mask."

She screamed at him to take it off, but he could not take it off. There was no longer anything to take off. Nixon had become one with the mask that wore him.

Introduction:

The Samhain Feis

BY PETER TREMAYNE

Peter Tremayne and his wife Dorothy live in a lovely Victorian house near Highgate Cemetery in North London. When he's not at The Flask, buying pints for American visitors, he's writing serious scholarly works on Celtic history, literature, and language. And when he's not doing *that,* he's writing colorful horror tales like *Zombie!, The Morgow Rises!,* and *The Curse of Loch Ness.*

For *Halloween Horrors,* I asked him to use his Celtic background for a tale set in Ireland. "The Samhain Feis" (pronounced SAH-WIN FESH) won't do much to promote tourism in the west of Ireland. It won't do much for New York suburbs, either.

The Samhain Feis

BY PETER TREMAYNE

Katy Fantoni began to wonder whether she had made a mistake almost as soon as she left the eastern suburbs of Dublin, taking the western road by the small airport at Rathcoole. Yet she had to get away from the stuffy city, away from the Victorian disapproval of Aunt Fand and her thin-lipped glances of reproach. She needed peace; a place to relax and work out her problem without the narrow-minded condemnation of her only relative.

It had been the local shopkeeper, a kindly woman, who had suggested that Katy might like to stay in the holiday cottage which she owned up in the Slieve Aughty Mountains in County Clare. At first the idea of spending a week in a remote country area was attractive to Katy, especially with the alternative being a week with Aunt Fand. But now, as she drove the hire-car through Kildare, misgivings began to tumble through her mind. After all, what was she going to do in a remote cottage in an alien countryside except brood . . . brood about Mario and her busted marriage?

She glanced into the driving mirror and caught sight of her seven-year-old son, Mike, sitting quietly on the back seat playing with his teddy bear. Was it fair to him, she wondered? He had been restless staying in Aunt Fand's house but, in her eagerness to escape Aunt Fand, had she precipitated them into a worse situation? It was to be a whole week in the isolated country cottage. She tried to dispel the disquiet from her mind with a shake of her fair hair. No, she refused to turn back now. Something urged her onwards, perhaps pride. She had already earned the disfavour of Aunt Fand; no need to give her another example of what the old woman saw as her niece's fecklessness.

Katy Fantoni—or rather, Katy Byrne, as she was then—had

been born in Dublin but, when she was five years old, her parents had emigrated to America and she had grown up in the Jamaica Bay area of Brooklyn. There was nothing special about her childhood; it was a common story of most immigrant Irish families. Not long after she had graduated from high school and secured a job in an advertising agency, however, her parents were killed in an automobile accident. Then she had met Mario Fantoni. Mario managed a chain of diners, owned by his father, Salvatore Fantoni, on Long Island. It was whispered that Salvatore Fantoni was "connected" . . . a euphemism for membership in the Mafia. Katy Byrne's agency was owned by Gentile Alunno and it was doing a campaign for the Fantoni diners. That was how they met.

Mario was young, handsome, and good company. Katy was young, attractive, and very much alone with an emotional vacuum since the death of her parents. To both Katy and Mario, with their Catholic backgrounds, marriage was the next step. Mama and Papa Fantoni were not exactly happy that Mario was not marrying "Italian," for they were Sicilians of an archaic type. But they consoled themselves with the fact that Katy Byrne was a good Catholic.

So Katy and Mario were married. Mama and Papa Fantoni bought them a house in Glen Cove, overlooking Long Island Sound. It was a large house and with it came Lise, a good-natured though coarse-looking Calabrian, who was the housekeeper. A year later they had a son, Mike. Katy mentally prepared herself to settle down to an indolent life. After all, working for his father, Mario Fantoni had no financial worries.

The honeymoon did not last long. As soon as Katy became noticeably pregnant she began to learn some unpleasant truths about Mario. Mama and Papa Fantoni had brought him up in some old-fashioned Sicilian philosophies where wives were concerned. Even after Mike was born Katy was expected to stay home, act as hostess at a moment's notice when Mario decided to invite his friends to drop in, and not to develop any friendships of her own. Mario was always out on "business dates" and it soon came to Katy's knowledge that his business colleagues were all about twenty years old, came in a variety of colourings and just one gender—female! When she contemplated her seven years with Mario, Katy did not really understand how the marriage had survived that period. She supposed it was unconscious pressure from her Catholic upbringing. Or maybe she had been waiting for Mario to mature, waiting for him to change . . .

Then Mario went off on a West Coast tour "strictly for business" . . . and Katy was not long in discovering that the business sessions were taking place in Las Vegas night spots and motels and that his travelling companion was some TV starlet. That was when her Irish blood finally boiled over and she hopped a plane for Dublin with little Mike in tow, telling Lise that she would return in a couple of weeks—probably!

Katy Byrne Fantoni had one surviving relative and that was Aunt Fand in Dublin. She was the elder sister of Katy's mother, and while they had exchanged cards from time to time, Katy had not seen her since she was five years old. She had thought to find in Aunt Fand some of her mother's caring nature, her broadmindedness and concern. Instead Aunt Fand was a bigot as only a spinster of fanatical religious disposition can be. Ostentatious piety was a substitute for Christian charity. Her narrowness was demonstrated by her enthusiastic support of Archbishop Lefevre, who refused the introduction of the modern vernacular Mass in his churches as being impious and adhered strictly to the sixteenth-century Latin Mass. Aunt Fand's ideas on divorce were more extreme than those of the Pope. She was parochial and narrow and threw up her hands in horror when Katy began to speak of her problems with Mario and hinted she was contemplating a legal separation. Aunt Fand was hardly the person to confide in.

After the first week living in Aunt Fand's house in the small Dublin suburb of Kimmage, Katy was feeling stifled and oppressed. Even young Mike asked her one bedtime whether Aunt Fand was their wicked stepmother. Katy had taken the boy to see Disney's *Cinderella* a few days before.

Katy felt that she just had to escape in order to think quietly and rationally about her situation.

It was when she was in the local grocery store and fell to talking with Mrs. MacMahon, the owner, that she mentioned she would like to get away for a few days to the west of Ireland. Mrs. MacMahon promptly suggested that Katy might like to stay in a holiday cottage which she owned in County Clare.

Katy hesitated out of a certain respect for Aunt Fand's hospitality before agreeing.

"It's up in the Slieve Aughty Mountains," smiled Mrs. MacMahon. "Near Lough Atorick. All you have to do is take the main road from Dublin to Portumna, drive past Lough Derg, turn south on the Ennis Road; turn off at Gorteeny for Derrygoolin, and then ask for Flaherty's farmstead. Ned Flaherty keeps the keys of the cottage and he'll let you in. There's a trackway from his farm which winds up into the mountains and you'll find the cottage by the lakeside about ten miles further on."

Ned Flaherty was a man of indeterminate age. He had snow-white hair, a shrewd weatherworn face, and sparkling deep blue eyes, almost violet in colour. Humour never seemed to be far from his features.

When Katy drove up to the farmstead, found him, and handed over Mrs. MacMahon's scribbled note giving her permission to stay at the cottage, Flaherty was clearly astonished. He looked from Katy Fantoni to young Mike in surprise.

" 'Tis late for tourists," he said in his slow, rolling County Clare drawl.

"I'm not really a tourist," Katy replied. "I just want a few days of quiet in a remote spot."

He frowned. "And you an American?" he pondered. "Well, peace and quiet you'll be getting up at the croft and that's no lie."

He turned into the farmhouse and reappeared with a bunch of keys. "I'd best come and show you the croft."

He climbed into the car beside her and directed her up a track, a single unpaved trackway that twisted itself into the mountains. It was obvious that this track was rarely used. Now and then they had to halt and push their way through sheep who stood indifferent to the angry blasts of the car horn. As they climbed upwards the scenery became spectacular. Katy had always believed that Ireland was at its best in the golds, russets, and muted greens of autumn. The gorse-strewn mountains were speckled in pale yellow.

Suddenly they came round the shoulder of a mountain onto a high plateau, a small valley with a large lake in its centre. By the lakeside stood a quaint thatched cottage with thick grey stone walls.

"Mrs. MacMahon's croft," gestured the old farmer with a jerk of his head.

She halted the car before the cottage, or croft as Flaherty called it, and the dismay must have registered on her face.

The croft was fronted with a garden, bordered by a low stone wall of the same grey granite as the house. The garden had become overgrown and wild.

"It's a lonely spot, right enough," Flaherty said, observing her expression. "No gas, no electricity, nor a telephone."

Her spirits fell. "What shall I do for light and heat?"

"There's oil lamps, a fire, and plenty of turf, and there'll be a primus stove as well for the cooking. I'll show you."

She sighed as she climbed out of the car and followed him to the cottage door. Little Mike was running after them in ecstasy.

"Look, Mommy! Look! Can I play here? Is it ours?"

Well, it was certainly a beautiful spot. "Isolated" was hardly the word for it, though. It seemed a million miles from anywhere. Flaherty seemed to read her mind.

"No one has lived here for many years. In winter, when it rains, the road gets cut off. The old croft was deserted until Mrs. MacMahon from Dublin bought it. She only comes for a fortnight in summer and then lets it from time to time. I've never known it to be occupied so late in the year, though."

Katy turned and gazed about her as he fiddled with the keys.

The sun shone on the lake which reflected the pale blue of the sky. It seemed pleasant and inviting. To the side of the croft the mountain rose to a black jagged peak, looking more like a hill from this elevation on the high plateau. It was strewn with granite boulders, poking up in grotesque shapes through the black earth. It was a strange landscape, almost out of a fantasy world.

Flaherty caught her gaze.

"That's *Reilig na Ifreann,*" he said.

"What does that mean?"

"The Cemetery of Hell."

Katy grinned.

"I see the likeness. The granite boulders do look a bit like tombstones."

They left little Mike racing around the garden, finding curious things to do.

"Keep in the garden, Mike," she admonished him as Flaherty conducted her inside. The door opened immediately into a large room which was apparently a combined kitchen, dining and living room. Two doors led off this large central room with its big open fireplace. One door led into a small bedroom which Katy immediately designated for Mike, while the other led into a larger bedroom which she took for herself. It was primitive but it was quaint. She knew many New York matrons who would pay a fortune to stay in such a place.

Flaherty proved to be a treasure. He laid a turf fire and lit it, showing her how to build it so that it would remain alight through the night. He showed her how the primus stove worked and how to light the oil lamps. The water was drawn by a pump which emptied into a big china sink. They managed to find a kettle and some tea bags and brew a cup of milkless, unsweetened tea.

"I'll have to collect some groceries from the village," Katy reflected.

Flaherty nodded.

"At least you have a car," he smiled. "In the old days one had to walk the twelve miles to the village and return the same way carrying the shopping."

"No wonder the place became deserted."

They finally climbed back into the hire-car and drove back down the mountain road. Once again Flaherty shook his head as he gazed at them.

"I've never known the croft to be let so late in the year," he said. " 'Tis almost the Samhain Feis." The words were pronounced "Sowan Fesh."

Katy gazed at him with a smile of puzzlement. "What's that?"

"Hallowe'en. We still call it by its old name in these parts."

Young Mike piped up from the back seat: "Mommy! Mommy! Are we going to have a Hallowe'en party with pumpkin masks and candles and games?"

"We'll see." Katy smiled at him in the driving mirror. "Do they have any local Hallowe'en celebrations in the village, Mr. Flaherty?"

Flaherty gave her a curious glance. "The Samhain Feis is not a time to celebrate," he replied in an almost surly manner.

"I thought everyone celebrated Hallowe'en," Katy said with raised brows. "In the States it's a great time for the kids."

Flaherty sighed deeply.

"Samhain, which you call Hallowe'en, is an ancient festival celebrated among the pagan Irish centuries before the coming of Christianity."

"Tell me about it," said Katy. "I'm interested, truly."

"Samhain was one of the four great religious festivals among the pagan Irish. It started on the evening of October 31 and continued on November 1. It marked the end of one pastoral year and the beginning of the next. The name is derived from the words *Samred,* meaning summer, and *fuin,* meaning the end. Hence it was 'end of summer,' for Samhain was the first day of *Gemred,* the winter. It was the time when, according to the druids, the Otherworld became visible to mankind and when spiritual forces were loosed upon the human race."

Katy chuckled. "So that is the origin of the Hallowe'en idea? The night when evil marches across the world, when spirits and ghosts set out to wreak their vengeance on the living?"

Flaherty simply stared, obviously not sharing her merriment.

"Christianity was unable to suppress many of the old beliefs. A great many pagan beliefs and superstitions and even ceremonies were adopted by the early Christians. Samhain was renamed All Saints' or All Hallows' Day so that the evening before became Hallowe'en."

Katy smiled. "You have quite a wealth of folkloric knowledge, Mr. Flaherty."

"When you live up in these mountains, the folk memory becomes an extension of your own experience."

Within two days Katy had settled in the area and even grown used to the primitive living conditions of the croft. As for little Mike, he loved playing in the garden. Ned Flaherty seemed to take them under his personal protection and was always calling by for a brew of tea. He was a natural storyteller and had an amazing wealth of knowledge on many subjects. The English he spoke was slow and sedate and apparently Irish was his first language. In fact, Irish seemed to be quite widely spoken among the remote mountain folk.

It was on the third day that Katy suddenly realised that she had not once thought about Mario. Mario! It was high time that she sorted that mess out. After all, it was her whole reason for being in Ireland. But she had been so engrossed with learning to live in primitive style, with listening to Flaherty's stories and walking amidst the wild countryside, that the problem of Mario seemed remote and almost nothing to do with her.

It was surprising. She could not even blame the distraction on little Mike, for the boy was no burden at all. He loved playing by himself and, indeed, invented an imaginary playmate with whom he seemed quite content.

One day when Katy was cleaning the kitchen he came running into the croft to tell her about his playmate.

"He's called Seán Rua, Mommy. That means Red John," added the little boy proudly.

Katy frowned, peering out of the window. "And where is this Red John?" she demanded.

Mike pointed to the garden gate. "There he is."

Katy could see nothing except a bird perched on the gate post, a bird which looked like a raven, although the sun made its black feathers glow with a curious coppery colour.

It was at that point that Katy realised the situation. She had had an imaginary friend when she was Mike's age; it was a phase all children went through.

"I see." She smiled and ruffled the boy's fair hair. "Well, you run off and play for a while because I'm going to fix your supper."

Dutifully, little Mike trotted off.

The next morning Mike was eager to play with his "friend" and so Katy left him with strict orders not to move out of the cottage garden while she went to pick up a few necessary provisions from the village. As she drove by Flaherty's farmstead she saw the old man sitting on a stone bridge which spanned a gushing mountain stream. He was gazing moodily up at the darkening rain-laden skies while whittling a stick. He smiled when he saw her, and waved, so she halted the car and wound down the window.

"Settling in?" he asked.

"No problems," she replied with a smile.

"And where is the *garsún?*"

Katy frowned. "The gosoon?" she echoed.

"The boy. Isn't he with you?"

"Ah, no. He's having a game around the cottage. He's invented an imaginary friend to play with. He calls him Seán Rua."

"Nár lige Dia!" whispered Flaherty, suddenly genuflecting with the sign of the Cross.

Katy gazed at his troubled face in surprise. "What's wrong?" she demanded.

"Nothing," muttered Flaherty. "Will you be out long?"

"I'm just going down to the village to buy a few things."

The old man peered at the sky. "You realise that it is the Samhain Feis tonight?"

Katy couldn't quite grasp the abrupt change of topic.

Flaherty stood up, nodded to her, and walked briskly towards his tractor.

When Katy returned to the croft she found Flaherty sitting on the stone wall of the garden, whittling his stick and watching little Mike as he attempted to dam a stream which ran through the overgrown wilderness. Katy thought that the old man was being a little overprotective.

"You shouldn't have bothered to watch over Mike," she said as she unloaded the car. "He wouldn't have come to any harm in the garden."

"Ah," shrugged the old man, "it's turned into a nice afternoon. The rain clouds have blown clear of the mountain and it's nice enough to sit in the sun."

Katy nodded absently as little Mike came running up. She had promised to bring him some sweets. As she handed him a toffee he said, "Mommy, may I have one for Seán Rua?" Inwardly she groaned. She would have to watch that. Imaginary friends were all right until two of everything was demanded. Just this once, she thought, as she handed Mike another toffee. He took them both and ran to the far side of the garden where he appeared to be in conversation with someone.

Flaherty, watching him, plucked at his lower lip thoughtfully.

"Strange that the *garsún* picked on that name," he mused. "There is an old tale hereabouts . . ."

"The whole place is riddled with old tales," Katy interrupted as she heaved her shopping bags to the cottage.

Flaherty followed.

"One of the beliefs of the Samhain Feis is that on the stroke of midnight the fairy hills split wide open and from each fairy hill there emerges a spectral host . . . goblins, imps, bogeymen, demons, phantoms, and the like. They spill out to take revenge on the living. The local people stay indoors on that night of the Samhain Feis."

Katy smiled tolerantly at him as she started to unpack. "What has that got to do with the name Mike chose for his playmate?"

"Of all the goblins and imps who appear at the Samhain Feis, there is a small red-haired imp called the *Taibhse Derg.*"

"The Tavesher Derug?" Katy tried to repeat the name. "What's that?"

"The Red Bogeyman," replied Flaherty solemnly. "Round these parts we call him Red John. It is said he eats the souls of children."

Katy glanced at the old man, not sure whether he was joking with her. Flaherty's face was grave.

"Tonight is the Samhain Feis, Mrs. Fantoni. Do you have a crucifix in the croft?"

Katy's jaw dropped a little. Then, trying to suppress a smile, she pointed above the cottage door where an ornate crucifix hung.

Flaherty nodded approvingly. "That's a good place to hang it," he said. "But would you take notice of an old man? Mix a paste of oatmeal and salt and put it on your child's head before he goes to bed tonight."

Katy could scarce keep from laughing. "What would that do, Mr. Flaherty, except make a mess for me to clean up?"

"It will keep the boy from harm," he replied solemnly. Then the old man wished her a "good night" and walked off towards his tractor.

Katy watched it trundle down the mountain path and suddenly realised how removed she had become from the superstitions of her Irish roots. The years in New York had taught her some sophistication. Oatmeal and salt indeed! Crucifixes! Goblins! Imps! The Samhain Feis!

A wild croaking made her peer upwards.

A flock of birds were wheeling around the roof of the cottage, their wings beating in the crisp air. She came out into the garden to stare upwards, attracted by their lamenting cacaphony. She knew enough of birds to recognise ravens by their appearance, although the lowering sun seemed to make their feathers flicker with a coppery glow. Three times she watched them circle overhead and then fly upwards towards the distant peaks of the mountains.

She turned into the croft again and continued to sort her groceries.

Katy had just finished cooking supper when she noticed the chill in the air and realised that the sun was already disappearing over the mountain tops. It was nearly time to light the lamps.

She looked through the window and saw young Mike standing at the garden gate. She gazed in surprise for he was with another small boy, a boy with bright coppery hair which flickered with a thousand little pinpricks of light in the rays of the setting sun. Katy hurried to the door and opened it.

Was she cracking up? Mike was standing by the gate alone. Katy peered round. There was no one about.

"Mike!" she called. "Time to come in now."

Mike turned and waved at the empty air and then trotted towards her.

"It's been a lovely day, Mommy." He smiled.

"Mike." Katy hesitated, feeling foolish. "Were you with a small red-haired boy just a moment ago?"

"Of course," came his prompt reply. "I was with Seán Rua."

Katy shuddered slightly. Perhaps she was cracking up?

"Seán Rua wants me to go out and play with him tonight because it's the Samhain Feis."

Katy pulled herself together. "Well, Mr. Fantoni Junior," she replied, "I am sure that young Seán Rua's parents will have him tucked up in bed tonight and that is where you are going to be."

Little Mike's lips drooped. "Aw, Mom!"

"No buts or complaints, it's bed for you at your usual time, young man."

Mike had finally settled to sleep in his room and Katy had put some more turf on the fire, then sat in the old carved chair before it, warming her feet and sipping a cup of hot chocolate. It was so peaceful, just sitting there with the music of the ticking clock on the mantelshelf and crackle of the fire in the hearth.

She supposed it was at that moment that she made up her mind finally about Mario Fantoni. It was ridiculous pretending that a relationship still existed. Separation or divorce was the only solution. Everything swam into crystal clarity. She set down her cup and sighed.

Abruptly she became aware that a curious thing had happened. A deathly silence pervaded the cottage. The loud ticking of the clock had stopped. The silence made her glance up in astonishment. It was one minute to midnight. She turned her eyes to the fire whose flames roared and crackled away . . . without any sound at all. God! Had she gone deaf?

Her heart began to beat wildly.

Then she heard a sibilant whispering which was incomprehensible at first but which grew in volume like the keening of a wind. It grew louder until she could hear the clear, melodic voice of a child.

"Mi-ike . . . ! Mi-ike . . . ! Come and play with me . . . come and play . . ."

She turned her head to see where the whispering came from.

The creak of a door caused her to start.

Across the room, the door of Mike's bedroom was swinging slowly open.

A shadow moved there.

Little Mike came stumbling forward, barefoot, clad in his striped pyjamas. His eyes were blurry and blinking from his sleep.

"Mi-ike! Mi-ike . . . come and play!"

She tried to stand up and found a great weight pressing her back in her chair. She tried to call out to Mike but her throat was suddenly constricted.

A sharp rasp of a bolt being drawn caused her to jerk her gaze over her shoulder towards the door of the cottage. She gazed fearfully as she saw the bolts being drawn back of their own volition! First one iron bolt and then the other was drawn aside, then the handle moved and the cottage door swung inwards.

The whispering voice grew louder.

"Mi-ike!"

Little Mike's eyes were wide open now and he was smiling.

"Seán Rua!" he cried. "I knew you would come for me. I want to play, truly I do."

Katy struggled to free herself from her strange paralysis while Mike, ignoring her, went trotting trustingly towards the door.

Katy turned her frantic gaze after him.

Just beyond the cottage door she could see the shadowy outline of a little boy.

Then a great chanting chorus filled the air and the earth seemed to quiver and shake under the cottage. It rocked as if there was an earthquake.

Through the open door she could see the outline of the oddly shaped peak which Flaherty had called *Reilig na Ifreann*—Hell's Cemetery.

Even as she watched, the earth seemed to spring apart as if opening a jagged tear down the side of the mountain. A pulsating red light shone forth into the night. The chanting grew exhilarated, increasing in volume until Katy felt her eardrums would burst with the vibration.

She saw Mike's little figure run through the doorway, saw the shadowy figure behind awaiting him with outstretched hand.

The light from the open hillside seemed to glow on the figure's red coppery hair, causing it to dance as if it were on fire. And the light from the cottage fell onto its face.

Oh God! That face!

Malevolent green eyes stared unblinking at her from slanted, almond shapes. The face was deathly white and its contours were sharp. The eyebrows also rose upwards. The cheekbones were sharp and jutting and the ears were pointed, standing almost at right angles to the head. It was an elfin head.

For a moment the face of the creature—what else was it?—stared at Katy and then, slowly, a malicious smile crossed those bizarre features.

Little Mike ran straight up to it, their hands grasped each other, and then the two tiny figures turned and ran towards the opening in the mountainside.

Katy's wildly beating heart increased its tempo until she could stand its beat no longer and fell into a merciful world of blackness.

She awoke still sitting in the chair, twisted uncomfortably before the dead fire. The oil lamp was spluttering and smelling on the table behind her. The room was terribly cold and the grey half-light of dawn seeped through the small windows of the croft.

She raised her itching eyes to the monotonously ticking clock. It was seven-thirty. She eased herself up, stretched, and stared at the dead embers of the fire.

Then she remembered.

Her eyes swung to the door of the croft. It was closed. The bolts were in place and nothing seemed out of order. She sprang from her chair and turned towards Mike's room. The door was closed. She hesitated before it, scared of what she might find on the other side.

Summoning her courage, she turned the door knob and peered in.

Mike's tousled fair head lay on the pillow, a hand to his mouth, thumb inserted between his lips. His breathing was deep and regular.

Katy could have wept with relief.

She turned back into the main room, shivering.

So it had been some grotesque nightmare after all? She must have fallen asleep in front of the fire and had the strangest dream! She supposed it was a mixture of fears; fears about Mike, her own fears . . . and all restated through Flaherty's folk tales. She shook her head in disgust and set to building a fire. She had just set the primus stove going when she heard the sound of Flaherty's tractor halting outside.

"I was just passing," the old man said when she opened the door. "I thought I'd call by . . ."

"I'm making tea." Katy smiled as she gestured him to enter.

His bright eyes gazed keenly at her.

"You seem tired," he observed.

"I fell asleep in front of the fire last night," she confessed, "and had a rather nasty nightmare."

He pursed his lips thoughtfully. "How's the *garsún?*"

"Mike? He's sleeping."

"Ah."

Katy glanced at the old man pityingly. She felt confident now in the morning light. "Well, your Samhain Feis is over. Did anyone get their souls eaten last night?"

Flaherty sniffed. " 'Tis not a thing to joke about. But, true, the Samhain Feis is over for another year, *búiochas le Dia* . . . thanks be to God," he added piously.

"Mommy!"

Katy turned as Mike came stumbling from his bedroom, yawning and rubbing the sleep from his eyes. "Mommy, I'm hungry!"

Flaherty slapped his thigh and laughed. "Now that's the sign of a healthy lad. Here, *a mhic,"* he called to the boy, "I've a little something for you."

He reached into his coat pocket and handed little Mike a length of wood, the same wood piece that Katy had seen the old man whittling so often. It had been transformed into a beautiful ornate whistle.

" 'Tis called a *feadóg stáin,* a penny-whistle," smiled Flaherty.

Mike held the whistle up and gave a few tentative blasts.

"Go raibh maith agat," he said solemnly to the old man.

Flaherty chuckled. *"An-mhaith! Is rómhaith uait é sin!"* He clapped the boy on the shoulder and turned to Katy. "I see you're making the boy fluent in Irish."

Katy frowned. "Not me. I don't know a word of the language. Where did you pick that up, Mike?"

"From my friend," smiled Mike, retiring to a corner to practise on the whistle.

Flaherty apparently did not hear, nor did he see the troubled look which passed across Katy's face. He sipped appreciatively at his tea.

"I shall miss the *garsún* and yourself when you leave."

Katy turned back to him and smiled. "That's a nice thing to say. We'll be going back to Dublin in a day or so and then straight back to New York."

The old man gazed shrewdly at her. "And the problem you came here to think about? Is it resolved?"

Katy smiled, a little tightly. "In my mind it is."

Flaherty sighed. "Then perhaps you'll come back here one day."

"Perhaps."

A week later the cab dropped Katy and Mike at the house in Glen Cove. Mario was home and he was drunk and angry at Katy's "disappearance." Almost before she stepped into the living room he started to scream abuse at her for taking *his* son out of the country without permission. He accused her of attempting to kidnap young Mike. Katy tried to keep calm; tried to keep her temper in check. In the end she let it all out: how she was sick of Mario's countless girl friends, his drunken boorish behaviour, his attitude towards her and, finally, how she was utterly sick of him and their relationship. She wanted a separation pending a divorce.

After his initial shock Mario grinned derisively. "You try to divorce me and I'll countersue," he sneered. "What's more, I'll make sure that enough mud is thrown at you to ensure the courts give me custody of Mike so that you'll never see him again. No one walks out on me, baby!"

Katy stared at him aghast.

There was no use asking if he meant it. She could see by the triumphant leer in his eyes that he meant every word and was capable of carrying his threat through. She knew exactly how much power the Fantonis could wield. He would take Mike from her not because he cared for Mike but in order to spite her. That was when she picked up a china ornament and threw it straight into Mario's grinning, triumphant face. He dodged aside easily and called her a string of foul names.

"I wish you were dead!" she snarled in reply. "I hope you rot in hell!"

She turned on her heel and found little Mike standing in the open doorway behind her. He was staring at his father with a curious expression on his face. There was a look of such malevolence in his eyes that it made Katy pause and shiver. Mario, too, saw the expression.

"Hey, kid, wipe that look off your goddamn face and show your old man some respect! Don't stare at me like that!"

Mike said nothing but continued to stare at his father.

Mario became really angry. "Hey, what stories have you been filling the kid's head with about me, you bitch?" he snarled at Katy. "Have you been feeding the kid with tales about me?"

"He only has to see the way you behave to know what kind of person you are," replied Katy evenly. "There's no need for tales."

Mario was staring at the boy's hair.

"Have you been dying the kid's hair?"

Katy frowned, not understanding what he meant at first. Then she glanced at Mike's hair. The fair tousled curls were much darker than usual, a deeper brown, almost chestnut. She blinked. Maybe it was the lighting in the room. The hair seemed to verge on copper in colour.

"Quit staring at me, kid!" shouted Mario, suddenly lunging towards the boy.

Katy did not know how it happened, but as Mario moved forward he somehow tripped and fell on his face.

She glowered down at him.

"You drunken bum!" she said through clenched teeth. "When you've sobered up, we'll talk about that divorce."

"I'll see you in hell first!" swore Mario from the floor.

Katy grabbed little Mike and hurried upstairs.

It was early the next morning when Lise, the housekeeper, woke Katy from a deep sleep. Her face was pale and she was in a state of agitation.

"Dio! Dio! Signore Fantoni è morto!"

Katy rubbed the sleep from her eyes and stared at the woman who was waving her arms, repeating the words in her broad Calabrian accent.

"What is it?" demanded Katy. "Is it Mike? Oh God, has something happened to Mike?"

"No, no." The woman shook her head between her sobs. "It is Signore Fantoni . . ."

"What's the matter?"

Lise was shivering hopelessly and pointed to the corridor.

Since their relationship became uneasy, Katy and Mario had separate bedrooms. Mario's bedroom lay across the corridor opposite.

Katy threw on a dressing gown and strode to Mario's door with Lise sobbing in her wake.

The first thing Katy noticed was the blood. It was everywhere, staining the room streaky red. Mario lay on his back on the bed amidst the jumble of bedclothes. His eyes were wide and staring as if in fear.

Katy raised a hand to her mouth and felt nausea well from her stomach.

It looked as if part of Mario's throat had been torn out.

Behind her Lise breathed, *"Animale! Lupo mannaro!"*

Katy paused a moment longer, drew herself together, and pushed Lise from the room before her. Outside, in the corridor, she felt shivery and faint.

"Call the police, Lise," she said. "Get a hold on yourself and get the police." Her voice was sharp and near hysteria.

Lise turned away.

"Mike!" Katy suddenly cried. "We must keep him away from this. Where is he?"

Lise turned back, sniffing as she tried to control herself. "He was playing when I started to make Signore Fantoni his breakfast. Just playing on the lawn, signora."

Katy strode to her bedroom window and gazed down on the lawn below.

Sure enough, there was little Mike playing; running round and round in circles on the lawn, the sun glinting on his coppery hair. Katy caught her breath. His *coppery* hair!

Almost as if he heard her sharp intake of breath, he stopped and gazed up at the bedroom window.

Katy's heart began to pump wildly and she clutched for the window sill.

It was little Mike's face right enough, yet the features were somehow distorted, sharper. The eyes were almost almond-shaped. The ears were pointed and stood out at right angles. The face was malignant, elfin. He stared up and his green sparkling eyes gazed into Katy's. Then he smiled. A shy, mischievous smile. And she noticed there was blood on his lips.

Introduction:

Trickster

BY STEVE RASNIC TEM

Steve Rasnic Tem sold his first short story to Ramsey Campbell's *New Terrors.* Since then he has won a reputation as one of the finest new writers of short stories in the field. The first significant display of his work was in my own anthology, *Night Visions 1,* which contained seven original stories.

A few years ago, Tem, like most other writers in the field of horror, attended the World Fantasy Convention over Halloween weekend in Berkeley, California. One night he left the hotel and went out to explore San Francisco. A writer like Tem tends to see things that other people don't see. Sometimes he even sees things that are (almost) not there.

Trickster

BY STEVEN RASNIC TEM

The giant green lizard with the hideous yellow tongue lapped greedily at our Volkswagen windshield. Marcie shouted and covered her face, her hand hitting the horn as she jumped.

Then she looked up again, laughing nervously. "That's quite a costume!" she said. I agreed. The crowd of Halloween revelers on Fisherman's Wharf walked around our car laughing, pointing, some of them grabbing the lizard's tail and giving it a shake. The lizard thrashed its head and roared.

"How do you think he does that trick with the tongue?" Marcie asked. "It looks so *real.*"

"I don't know. He's pretty good, almost as good as my brother was . . ." The man in the lizard costume was staring at me through the eyeholes. I could almost feel his gaze. Pressing closer to the windshield, I looked into his eyes. And I swear to you . . . they were my brother's eyes. My dead brother's eyes.

I shouted something and the lizard leaped off the hood of our car and strolled casually into the crowd. I opened the door quickly and ran after him. I heard Marcie yelling, but I ignored her. I was close now; I couldn't let him get away.

Halloween, the great witch night, was a favorite holiday for my brother Alex and me, although for different reasons. For me it was a somber time, a day and a night to dwell on those people I'd known who had died. I believed that in some way they would come back—and not necessarily as ordinary ghosts. Maybe as a shadow, a phrase in a letter that strikes you oddly, an old toy. But I was always the serious one, the thinker, never more than half child. My brother was the joker; Halloween for him was an excuse for the most outrageous kind of macabre jokes and theatrics.

Bright red hair, luminous gray eyes, that grin. Our mother used to say he was "purely half devil."

For me the spirits always seemed closer on Halloween night. For him the souls of the dead were actually walking.

He'd been gone a year; a year ago someone crushed his skull with a pipe. It happened in a side street in the Castro, gay turf in San Francisco. About three in the morning, the investigating officers said. The killer, or killers, had worked on him until the clown mask he'd been wearing became virtually a part of his face; at first the cops thought he'd just passed out drunk, until one of them bent down and touched what they thought was part of the glistening clown paint. My brother loved being a clown.

At first I didn't believe he was really dead. Why should I? It wasn't the first time. Three years ago I found him in a bathtub in his apartment, a smoke-blackened heater in the water with him, his face pale, beginning to turn blue. I squeezed back into the corner behind the sink, too terrified to touch him. Then he calmly stood up in the water and asked me for a towel.

He'd always been a trickster—even as a child. Not content to be a mere practical joker, he played with death.

It started with snakes and spiders, the usual thing, dropping them down girls' dresses and laughing when the girls went squealing to the teacher. But after a time he began adding a trick or two of his own: eating the spiders while the girls withered before him, carrying dead lizards around in his pockets for days in the hot summers. He was fascinated by such things, and even more fascinated by people's reactions to them.

I remember once when the family was on a picnic, having a good time. We heard him screaming and looked up just in time to see him toppling off the edge of the Powell River bridge. I thought our mother was going to die of fright. We ran over and found him hanging on a cable under the bridge, laughing at us.

Another time, he built an electric chair. It was an old barber's chair I'd helped him haul from the dump. He rigged it up with all sorts of fake electrical gear: glass insulators and broken meters and the like. Then he turned a steel bowl into a helmet and asked me to wear it while he snapped a picture. He strapped me into the chair with some old belts . . . to make it look more authentic, he said. After I was in place he suddenly pulled out a live wire from behind the chair and moved to insert it into a clip he had attached to the top of the steel helmet. I squirmed and screamed, almost hysterical. I really believed he was going to do it. He had maneuvered behind me; I couldn't see what he was doing. Then he came around in front of me with the wire again, and slid it into the clip.

Nothing. He had switched the wires. He held up the severed end of the wire he'd inserted into my helmet and grinned. He didn't laugh, didn't even giggle. He just grinned. I'll never forget it. One tooth missing and his eyes crinkling like those of some demented fairy.

Finally, when he was fourteen, Alex went too far. One of my mother's cousins, her husband, and new baby came to visit. We knew about a week ahead of time and Alex spent most of that week complaining about how he didn't want to see them and that he hated babies. He said that, if they came, something terrible would happen, said it in a threatening tone. That got him sent to his room. He obviously didn't mind; he had work to do there.

When her cousin's family arrived, Mother just couldn't stop fussing over the baby—how cute it was, how contented it looked. Alex sulked and made several rude remarks that almost got him sent to his room again. But he knew just when to stop.

They left the baby in the spare bedroom for a nap and the rest of us gathered for dinner. Except Alex. Mother called and called but he didn't answer. Dad looked as if he were ready to strangle him if he ever showed up.

Then we heard the baby crying.

Dad took one look at my mother and bolted from his chair. The rest of us followed. When we got to the bedroom door, it was locked. We could all hear my brother laughing on the other side of the door.

I'd never seen such fear on my father's face. He made me afraid too. For the first time I realized he really didn't trust my brother. He really thought Alex was capable of anything.

It was the baby's father who broke the door down.

We crowded through the doorway. Alex was there by the bassinet, grinning that weird grin of his. He was holding a knife. There was blood on it.

Mom's cousin ran to the bassinet. And screamed. I could see it from where I was standing. There was blood all over the blanket.

Her husband was the first to move. He leaped across the room and before anyone knew it had my brother on the floor, punching the daylights out of him. Dad and I tried to pull him off, but he wouldn't let Alex go until my brother's face was covered with blood. He still has—or had—a couple of scars and a slightly lopsided nose as a reminder of that day.

It was another joke, of course. Dad picked up the doll Alex had painted so gorily and flung it on the floor.

I stared at that doll for a long time. I was amazed. My brother had done a wonderful job—it looked so *real.* In an odd way, I found myself envying him.

They did send my brother away that time. For a month. He wasn't much different when he got back.

I couldn't run through the crowd of costumed figures—the sidewalks were packed. It was like wading through the images in some overcrowded dream brought on by too much drugs and alcohol. Demons and fairies and cowboys and giant bumblebees, talking pumpkins and Mr. Peanut. Three Mr. Peanuts, actually, maneuvering away from each other angrily. We can't all be originals, I suppose. I couldn't find the green lizard anywhere.

I ducked into Ripley's Believe It or Not. It was a hunch, but not a farfetched one. My brother had loved that sort of thing—oddities, deformities. I could hear Marcie's voice somewhere behind me, but I couldn't stop.

There weren't too many people in there. I guess there were enough oddities out on the sidewalk for them.

I saw it almost immediately. It was as if I had been drawn to it.

The doll my brother had made in his fourteenth year. Good as new, the fake blood glistening wetly beneath the bright lights. I had to stick my fingers in it; I couldn't help it. No, not quite the same. This time the blood was real.

I never really understood why I bothered with him, why I was so obsessed with him. I was always pulling him out of scrapes, bailing him out of jail, making excuses for him—to my parents, friends, everyone. Not that he cared for me—I don't remember him ever showing the slightest sign of affection, despite all that I'd done for him. One of his jokes cost me a job—he'd drugged me and driven me to work at the chemical plant, acting hysterical and telling my boss that the poisons we were making had finally gotten to me, and how he was going to make sure the plant was closed down. I can imagine the scene: all those men I worked with trying to get my dead body away from my crazed brother, and him finally pulling a loaded gun to hold them off. They never believed I had nothing to do with it.

But I still thrilled to his audacious exploits. I was the dull one, the careful one, the one easily embarrassed. I had trouble speaking my mind about most things. I was afraid to do anything out of the ordinary. He could act out things I could only feel. And secretly, I cheered him on.

"Come on now, you hate it when Dad drags us hunting!" Alex grinned his grin. Like a mask—it prevented you from seeing what he was really feeling.

"I know . . . but we . . . you can't do this."

"Just watch me, brother." He took the liver and raw meat scraps and laid them out carefully on our sleeping dog. He had sworn that the stuff he'd given Buck wouldn't hurt him, just make him sleep, and the old dog did seem to be breathing regularly—but you had to look close; from the doorway he looked dead, and with all that blood and raw meat—torn up something awful.

It was true; I didn't like going hunting with Dad. He'd shoot every game animal in sight, and throw away more than half of everything he killed. None of us enjoyed eating squirrel, dove, or deer, not even him. He just liked the shooting.

Once he'd made fun of me for refusing to shoot a bird. Said I was growing up too slow—that hunting was a great way to build character and that I was missing a golden opportunity. Then he laughed at the way I looked when he put the rifle in my hands. That was the only time I remember ever actually hating my father. I thought about that as I laid his hunting rifle down by our dog. My father loved that dog.

We waited behind the garage. I remember my brother grinning—a skull-grin, a rictus—as my father's car pulled up to the garage.

My father screaming. My brother grinning. And my own quiet satisfaction.

I ran outside, into a virtual wall of people in animal masks: monkeys and bats, parrots and cats and dogs, the hideous face of a deranged rhino. The people wore evening dress with their masks, which made their grotesque heads even more hideous. I thought about Samhain, Lord of the Dead, and Druids sacrificing animals before him. For a crazy moment I thought there might be truth in that old story: that if I ripped the animal masks from these people's faces I would find the same animal face beneath. They were the dead, walking among us, doomed to walk the earth in animal form until midnight tomorrow night, when Lord Samhain would harvest them with one great sweep of his gigantic, terrible scythe. I could hear someone laughing in their midst. Alex's laugh. A glimpse of a wide, luminous grin, one tooth missing. I twisted away from the crowd, ran into the street to avoid them. I couldn't bear the thought of touching even their fancy clothes.

A car stopped with a screech behind me. I turned and stared at the windshield. Then down at my knees, inches from the bumper. I thought I was going to cry, until Marcie jumped out from the driver's side, grabbed me, and pushed me into the car.

She was quiet for a long time. She was always patient with me; she was patient now. But she was angry. She tossed her head irritably and the shadows of black hair flowed, then settled down around her shoulders.

"Want to tell me about it?" she asked quietly.

"Alex. It was Alex. In the lizard suit."

She didn't sigh; she held on to it. "I really wish you wouldn't do this to yourself. I . . . know it's hard, but this is going to drive both of us crazy." Then, "Your brother's dead, Greg."

"I know he is," I said immediately, not even thinking about it. Then I thought about it, and I *was* convinced he was dead. But maybe he was waiting around now, after death. Waiting to be harvested . . .

I didn't see my brother much after high school. Occasionally there'd be an odd letter, or a strange picture or cryptic message in the mail. Sent anonymously, like some communication from the dark side of myself. But I always knew who sent the things; who else would do something like that? Once it was a picture of a woman working in a bomb factory. He had pasted a cartoon balloon next to her mouth saying: "I eat my dead children." Another time it was a shrunken head. I was afraid to get it authenticated.

I do know he dropped out, or was kicked out, of several colleges for his usual range of pranks. I know he got one midwestern fraternity shut down and forever banned because of his term as pledge master.

Then there was the letter to my parents, a sincere letter on the surface, confessing that he was gay. I didn't care, but of course my parents did. I've always wondered how much truth was in that letter—I suppose his usual haunts in the Bay Area would confirm the story, but it would be hard to tell with Alex. I suspect he was bisexual, considering his penchant for experimentation. Or maybe asexual. It's hard to imagine him loving, or even lusting after, anything more than he loved the dark and death.

It saddened me that I knew so little about my brother.

A few times as adults we did run into one another. One of the times was just after I'd married Marcie, and although we had sent him an invitation to the wedding it had been returned, marked addressee unknown.

We had just come back from a party in Berkeley. I walked into our bedroom—a little drunk, disoriented—and saw that there was a light on in the bathroom—I distinctly remembered turning that light out when we left the house. I stumbled in that general direction, and suddenly there was a deafening explosion at the back of my head and I fell unconscious.

It could be my imagination, but I have the distinct impression I saw my brother's face as I went down: narrow and skeletal, grinning.

Marcie told me later that when she went into the room she was struck by this awful smell, as if an animal had died in our bedroom. Then a soft voice—she thought it was my voice—said *come to bed; I need you, Marcie.* She walked over and switched on the bed table lamp and there I was lying on top of the covers, obviously dead, my skin peeling, my body reeking of corruption. She screamed and the light went out.

It was Alex, of course. When I came to, he was still in makeup; for my benefit, I suppose. His skills had definitely improved since our teen years: he looked just like me, identical to me, only dead. My stomach turned.

"Just thought I'd congratulate you and the missus, brother!" That was all he had to say.

Marcie started screaming at him. "Get out! Get *out!* What kind of sick *thing* are you, anyway? Why don't you crawl back into your slimy grave and leave *normal* people alone! Is that why you did this to us? Is that the only way you can get close to people?"

Then something odd happened. My brother stripped off his

makeup and just stared at her. I'd never seen such hatred, such revulsion, in his face before. His face took on almost an animal aspect—a wolf or a coyote. But then it changed into something else. Loss, or disappointment—I don't know—but he suddenly seemed such an outsider, something so alien, that my heart went out to him for an instant as it never had before. He got up and walked silently out of the house. Wraithlike. We didn't even hear the outer door open and close. It was as if he had never been there.

Marcie drove me away from Fisherman's Wharf, fighting her way through the goblins and witches, the bees and frogs that had gathered around us, up to the Cliff House restaurant overlooking the ocean. I discovered that I couldn't quite look at her, and instead kept turning to look out at the waves pummeling the rocky island a short distance offshore, and back to the other tables: bowls full of apples and nuts, a man in a cockroach suit, a woman wearing sequins glued to her cheeks in elaborate, spirograph patterns, and a man in a clown mask who seemed to be by himself, staring at me. The mask had blue gauze pasted over the eyeholes so he could see me, but I couldn't see his eyes, just two blue ovals.

I couldn't take my eyes away from him the second time I looked his way. No one was serving him. It was as if no one else saw him. Then Marcie touched my arm.

"Talk to me," she said.

"He's still alive." It was all I could say. The man in the clown mask still stared at me. Under the dim light in the corner he looked like an old photograph, yellowed and cracking, the surface of the photograph beginning to flake away from its backing. He still hadn't been served. The waitress walked right by him.

At the next table a group of people in peasant costumes and elegant masks were playing a fortune-telling game with cups of water, potato chips, and dirt. A beautiful blonde wearing a silk blindfold was feeling the outside of each cup, trying to decide in which one to put her fingers. There was a flowerpot behind them; I supposed that's where they'd gotten the dirt. One of the waitresses glanced at them, frowning.

"Greg, I know you're upset . . ."

I looked at her. "I'm sorry, but that was him . . . or what's left of him. He's waiting."

"What's he waiting for, Greg?"

"I don't know, but I think it's me . . ."

I looked away, trying to look at the ocean, the waves breaking, then looked back at the room and saw the grin, the wide glowing grin, one tooth missing. Alex was sitting where the clown had been.

I leaped out of my chair and stumbled past the drunken costumed figures at their tables. I reached for the grin, tripped, and crashed into the fortune-telling party: I looked down at my hand in the cup of dirt. When I looked at the table where the clown had been, a huge jack-o'-lantern sat there, almost covering the small tabletop, a candle behind the enormous grin, flickering, creating shadows. I grabbed the waitress who had come to help me.

"The man who was there . . . at that table . . . the clown mask . . ." I gasped.

She looked at me nervously and pulled away. "No one sat here tonight. This is my station. The pumpkin, you know? We put the pumpkin on this table."

Marcie got me out to the car, holding me up when I stumbled. Several people grinned at us, thinking I was drunk, I suppose. I kept turning back to the restaurant, the dark line of ocean, looking, looking. And just before Marcie shoved me into the passenger seat I saw the clown again, standing on the cliff beside the restaurant, taking off his mask.

And revealing another mask, a white glistening face, beneath it.

Marcie was quiet for most of the drive back into town. Then she glanced over at my dirt-encrusted hand. "You got pretty dirty there. What were they doing with those cups, anyway?"

"Fortune-telling," I said, staring at the road, waiting for something, anything to cross the path of the speeding car. I had the unnerving sensation of shadows in my peripheral vision. "You normally use dishes: one of water, one of meal—they used potato chips—and one of dirt. The one you put your fingers in reveals your destiny."

"And dirt? What is that supposed to mean?"

"Death," I said.

Marcie and I lived on Irving Street, down by Golden Gate Park. A small apartment, but I loved the location. I jogged every morning in the park and took walks through the gardens. When she pulled in to the curb, I reached over and covered her hand with the keys in it. "I want to drive around the park," I said quietly. "Just a few minutes before bed."

She looked at me. There were tears in her eyes. "You scare me, Greg."

"I'm okay, really." I leaned over and kissed her. "I just need to be by myself a little bit. Really, I'm fine." She waited on the street until I'd pulled around the corner.

I drove down Lincoln and parked near a Mohawk station on Ninth. Then I got out and walked. I'm always struck by the defensive nature of San Francisco architecture, particularly at night: security garage doors, bars on the windows, and a flight of steps leading up to the heavy entrance door. Bay windows on each side. I passed house after house like that, long rows of them. Like well-mannered old people on armored stilts, afraid of being bitten.

Golden Gate Park is not a good place to be at night. It's pitch dark, and if you hear a movement in the undergrowth you can never be sure if it's an animal or someone ready to deprive you of your money or life. I knew my brother had lived there, in the park, for three months one time, wandering around at night, sometimes leaping out in front of cars driving on Lincoln or one of the other bordering streets. He'd said it was one of his favorite places.

I thought of it as his favorite haunt.

I entered the park at Ninth and walked past the flower gardens. Then I turned toward the science museum.

A hill rose on my right, shrouded in trees and undergrowth. Like a neolithic burial mound, I thought, and I wouldn't have been surprised if some small misshapen fairies had climbed down out of the trees and carried me off.

I stopped at the giant bust of Beethoven. I looked up; I couldn't make out most of his features in the dark, but I could see that he was grinning.

When I turned and looked behind me, there was a fire in Tiffany Square.

It became clearer as I crossed the street and headed down the steps leading into the square. Someone had piled up leaves and wood and built a bonfire. I walked around it; there was no one there. There was a few wooden chairs burning, charring to ash, and what looked like an upside-down cross, or maybe it was just a broken piece of wood.

Pumpkins were scattered around the fire, as if they had been dropped in flight, their grins cracked or shattered. *At midnight all the pumpkins leave their vines and dance merrily across the field* . . . It was from an old story, or a song; I couldn't remember. I thought about the pumpkin farms at Half Moon Bay and wondered what surprises might be happening there that night.

Hey, brother . . .

I thought I heard it, but perhaps it was the fire chasing the leaves with slow explosions. There was a basket, or a wicker cage, lying among some of the pumpkins, something black inside. Something burned.

I crouched low and held my hand over my mouth.

Hey, brother . . .

It was a black cat, had been a cat. Raw red skin where the fur had burned away, eyes like red jelly.

Hey, brother . . .

I ran out of the park. The wind had picked up; a dog, something, scurried out of my way. The city lights made a milky nimbus over the treetops. I don't remember starting the car. I was already on Union, miles away, before I realized what I was doing.

Then I saw the orange glow in the rearview mirror, the jack-o'-lantern grinning through my back window. I could feel the heat of my brother's eyes in the glowing holes.

I shot up the first steep turnoff, the engine straining, whining in my ears. Crazy. As if I could outrun the apparition. But every time I looked into the rearview mirror it was still there, its grin burning brighter each time I looked. My hands were wet, even in the cold air of the car, and I felt the slightest pull, left sometimes, then right, as if something were fighting for possession of my hands on the wheel.

Dropping down Lombard Street, I sweated out each tortuous bend, wondering what could have possessed me to go onto that street—"the crookedest street in America," a street only the curious tourist would drive—faster and faster, until the bumpers were scraping the low walls separating that serpent of a street from the flower beds planted in the loops. Something jerked the wheel out of my hands and I screamed as the car slalomed down several more streets and I began to fall asleep, losing my grip on the steering wheel, hearing my brother whispering to me . . . news of his latest trick . . .

I woke up in the Castro, near where my brother was murdered. The pumpkin was gone from the back window. The car wouldn't start—dead. I would have to get out and walk.

I started checking out bars—I don't know why—maybe looking for a grinning face with bright red hair, maybe a guy in a clown mask. I wasn't stared at when I entered those places, much to my surprise. As if they'd seen me before, as if I were a regular. As if I belonged there. A leather shoulder turning. An eye deepened with blue mascara. A little rear-end cleavage. Hips sliding away to let me into the bar. A rattle of chrome-plated chains.

Things were different down in the Castro, Polk Street, this Halloween. The punk kids roving the streets in previous years had driven Halloween quietly indoors. And Ernie of Cliff's Variety Store had died, ending the annual costume contest on the huge stage in front of the store. The cops had little to do. They'd find more rowdiness among the jet set at the Cinderella Ball at the Mark Hopkins Hotel.

I found the place—thought I'd found the place—where Alex was murdered. I wasn't sure; at the time I hadn't come down to the site. I identified his body at the morgue. It *had* been his body, hadn't it?

"You aren't playing with me now, Alex? Are you?" I whispered into the wet gray mouth of the alley.

I could hear rats scurrying inside. Then glimpses of . . . something far back in the alley, occasionally catching the street light. Fur . . . claws . . . a wolf mask . . . a raven's head. "Alex?"

I heard a bell. Low and full, mournful.

A soul cake, a soul cake . . .
Have mercy on all Christian souls
For a soul cake . . .

The crier stepped out of the dark alley, ringing his bell. He was dressed in blacks: soot black, lamp black, dark black of the soul . . . I giggled nervously. He had the clown mask on.

"Alex?"

Hey, brother . . .

He walked up the street. I followed him. He pulled a piece of bread out of his dark costume and began to munch on it.

a picnic in the cemetery, brother . . .

He passed through a band of shadow and I heard bells tinkling. He turned, in a jester's costume now, white face, black grinning lips.

a soul can be helped through purgatory,
brother . . .

He went down another alley, and I followed. He turned into a doorway, stepping soundlessly through the trash, and I followed.

It was a small room. Dark. The figure sitting on the edge of the bed turned its face toward me and the halo of city fire outside the window caught the pale flat cheekbones, the bright red hair. He held out his arms, as if to embrace me.

"Another trick, Alex?"

But the figure on the bed stared at me sadly. He wasn't grinning now. There was such . . . loss . . . in those dull eyes. My heart went out to my brother, my aimless, wandering brother. Alone even in death. I let my heart go out to him, let myself love him at that moment. I couldn't know . . . he was still doing it to me . . .

And suddenly it was me on the bed. And my brother in my body, my disguise, standing in the doorway. Grinning his grin. His laughter was drawn-out, almost animal-like as he turned and walked away.

I couldn't move. I was frozen to the bed, fixed in shadow, and as night turned to day and the day ticked off into evening shadows again, a cool edge coming into the air, a silver edge to the black clouds in a blacker sky, I realized I was approaching the midnight of November 1, Lord Samhain's night. I felt increasingly . . . insubstantial, although when I looked at my reflection in the window I could still see a face—my brother's face—and the feral look it always had. The elongated jaw, wolf-like. Fox-red hair. The grin that would not go away, no matter how hard I tried. My brother was always the clever one, and I always envied him.

I could sense it coming, the great harvest. I was scared but could not leave the room.

Now . . . the black sky and that silver line. Now I can hear the swish of his great scythe . . .

Introduction:

Miss Mack

BY MICHAEL MCDOWELL

Michael McDowell attracted immediate attention with his first novel, *The Amulet*, a nasty bit of work set in his native south. Other novels followed, most notably the ghostly *Cold Moon over Babylon* and *The Elementals*, an extraordinarily disturbing nightmare bathed in, of all things, brilliant sunshine. Best known of his work is the six-volume family chronicle, *Blackwater*, a brilliant example of Southern gothic . . . with a vengeance. Currently—and in a lighter vein—he is working on a series of novels about a pair of perpetually young lovers named Jack and Susan.

"Miss Mack" is McDowell's first short story. Here he takes us back to his familiar Alabama landscape of Pine Cone, Babylon, and DeFuniak Springs, places that can be pretty strange even when it's *not* Halloween night.

Miss Mack

BY MICHAEL MCDOWELL

When Miss Mack showed up in Babylon in the late summer of 1957, nobody knew what to think of her. She had come from a little town called Pine Cone, and had a brother back there who did ladies' hair in his kitchen. Miss Mack was a huge woman with a pig's face, and short crinkly black hair that always looked greasy. Her vast shapeless dresses of tiny-patterned fabric seemed always to have been left too long in the sun. She always wore tennis shoes, even to church, because, as she candidly admitted, any other sort broke apart under her weight.

She wasn't old by any means, but a woman of such size and such an aspect wasn't regarded in the usual light, and nobody in Babylon gave any thought to Miss Mack's age. For seven years she had traveled all over Alabama, Georgia, and Florida, doing advance and setup work for the photographer who came in and took pictures of the grammar school children. She had been to Babylon before, on this very errand, and the teachers at the grammar school remembered her. Now the photographer was dead, and Miss Mack returned to Babylon. She showed the principal of the grammar school her college diploma and her teacher's certificate from Auburn University, and said, "Mr. Hill, I want you to give me a job."

Mr. Hill did it, not because he was intimidated, but because he had a vacancy, and because he knew a good teacher when he saw one.

Everybody liked Miss Mack. Miss Mack's children in the third grade adored her. Having inherited the itinerant photographer's camera, Miss Mack took pictures of every child in her class and pinned them to the bulletin board with their names beneath. Miss Mack's strong point was fractions, and she drilled her children relentlessly. Her weak point was Alabama history, so she taught them the state song, and let it go at that. On the playground, Miss Mack played with the boys. Infielders cowered and outfielders pressed themselves right up against the back fence when Miss Mack came to bat. At dodgeball, Miss Mack rolled the ball up inside her arm so tightly and so deep that it seemed buried in the flesh there. She unwound the ball so quickly and flung it so hard that the manliest boys in the center of the ring squealed and ducked. Miss Mack's dodgeball could put you flat out on the ground.

Because all teachers in the grammar school were called by their students "Miss," it was a matter of some speculation among her pupils whether or not she was married. When one little girl brought back the interesting report that Miss Mack lived alone in one of the four apartments next to the library, the children were all nearly overwhelmed with the sense of having delved deep into the mystery that was Miss Mack's private life.

Miss Mack's private life was also a matter of speculation among her fellow teachers at the grammar school. The first thing that was noticed was that, in Mr. Hill's words, she "kept the Coke machine hot," dropping in a nickel at every break, and guzzling down a Coca-Cola every chance she got. It appeared that Miss Mack couldn't walk down the hall past the teachers' lounge without sidling in with a nickel—she kept a supply in the faded pocket of her faded dress—and swilling down a bottle at a rate that could win prizes at a county fair. Miss Mack's apartment was not only next to the library, it was next to the Coca-Cola bottling plant as well. Wholesale, Miss Mack bought a case a day, summer and winter, and declared that, in point of fact, she preferred her Cokes warm rather than chilled.

Every weekend Miss Mack disappeared from Babylon. It was universally assumed that she drove her purple Pontiac up to Pine Cone to visit her brother, and maybe sit with him in the kitchen, swilling Coca-Cola while he fixed ladies' heads. But Miss Mack once surprised them all when she said that most weekends she went fishing. She drove all the way over to DeFuniak Springs because DeFuniak Springs had the best trout fishing in the world. She had a little trailer—the itinerant photographer's van with all the equipment jettisoned—parked on the side of some water there, and every weekend Miss Mack and three cases of Coca-Cola visited it.

Despite her alarming and formidable aspect Miss Mack quickly made friends in Babylon, and the friend she made earliest was the other third-grade teacher, Janice Faulk. Janice wasn't but twenty-two, just out of college, short and cute and always smiling. It was thought that Janice had a whole bureauful of white blouses with little puffed sleeves, because she was never seen in anything else. She wore little sweaters and jackets loosely over her shoulders, held in place by a golden chain attached to the lapels. Janice had loved every minute of her two years of teaching. Her children loved her in return, but tended to take advantage of her, because Miss Faulk could be wheedled into just about anything at all.

Mr. Hill, the principal, was even thinking of wheedling Janice into marriage. He had taken her down to Milton for pizza a couple of times, and they had gone to the movies in Pensacola, and he had asked her advice on buying a birthday present for his mother. Mr. Hill, a thin man with a broad smile, didn't think it necessary to say anything more just yet. When the time came he didn't doubt his ability to persuade Janice up to the altar. After all, he had hired her, hadn't he? And he had always made sure she got to teach the smartest and best-behaved kids, right? Janice was just the sort of impressionable young woman to imagine that such favors ought to be returned, with considerable interest. Mr. Hill had even told his mother of his intention of marrying Janice Faulk, and Mrs. Hill, a widow living in an old house in Sweet Gum Head, had heartily approved. Mrs. Hill in fact told her son he ought to propose to Janice without delay. Mr. Hill saw no need for haste, but a little later he was sorry not to have taken his mother's advice.

The next time Mrs. Hill spoke to her son on the subject of Janice Faulk—the following Halloween—Mr. Hill listened carefully. And he did exactly what his mother told him to do.

For what Mr. Hill hadn't counted on in his sanguine projection of easy courtship and easy marriage was the friendship of Janice and Miss Mack.

One Friday morning recess, the bully of Janice's class had fallen on the playground and split open his head on a rock. Janice had been about to run for Mr. Hill, but Miss Mack was right there, kneeling on the sandy ground, lifting the boy's head onto her lap, bandaging it as coolly as if she had been a trained nurse. Janice began to come to Miss Mack for other help and advice. Soon she was coming for the mere pleasure of Miss Mack's company. Janice's mother was dead, and her father worked five weeks out of six on an oil rig in Louisiana. She lived alone in a little clapboard house that was within sight of the grammar school. She visited Miss Mack in her apartment between the library and the bottling plant, and Miss Mack visited her in the lonely clapboard house. In Miss Mack's purple Pontiac they went to the Starlite drive-in. If they saw horror movies, Miss Mack held Janice's hand through the scary parts, and told Janice when it was all right to open her eyes. Miss Mack thought nothing of getting up from the supper table, and driving straight down to the Pensacola airport for the mere pleasure of watching the planes take off and land. On the four-lane late at night, Miss Mack came up right next to eighteen-wheel diesels, and made Janice roll down her window. Janice leaned her head cautiously out, and shouted up at the driver of the truck looking down, "You want to race Miss Mack?"

Miss Mack, in short, knew how to show a girl a good time.

By the summer after her first year of teaching, Miss Mack and Janice were inseparable friends, and an odd-looking pair they made. Miss Mack's appearance was vast, dark, and foreboding, and people in the street tended to get out of her way. She gave somewhat the impression of a large piece of farm machinery that had forsaken both farmer and field. Janice Faulk was petite, retiring, faultlessly neat, like the doll of a rich little girl—very pretty and not often played with. Both women, in consideration of the extra money and the opportunity to spend nearly all their time together, took over the teaching of all the summer remedial classes in the grammar and junior high schools. As if five days a week, all day long, were time insufficient to indulge the happiness they felt in one another's company, Miss Mack began taking Janice off to DeFuniak Springs every weekend.

Gavin Pond, left to Miss Mack by the itinerant photographer, was no more than five acres in extent, surrounded on all sides by dense pine forest. One end of the pond was much shallower than the other, and here a large cypress grove extended a dozen yards or so out into the water. The little trailer, still bearing the name and the promises of the itinerant photographer, was set permanently in a small clearing on the western edge of the pond. Directly across was a little graveyard containing the photographer, his ancestors, and his kin by marriage. A dirt track—no more than two gravel-filled ruts really—had been etched through the forest all the way around the pond. At compass-north it branched off toward the unpaved road, a couple of miles distant through the forest, that eventually led into the colored section of DeFuniak Springs. Altogether, Gavin Pond was as remote as remote could be.

Miss Mack and Janice arrived at the pond every Friday evening, having stopped on the way only for a coffee can of worms and a rabbit cage of crickets. They unloaded the car, fixed supper, and played rummy until ten, when they went to sleep. Next morning they rose before dawn, ate breakfast, prepared a lunch, and went out in the little green boat that was tethered to one of the cypresses. All morning long they fished, and piled up trout and bream in the bottom of the boat. Janice thought this great fun, so long as Miss Mack baited her hook and later removed the gasping fish from it. The two women beneath their straw hats didn't speak, and all that could be heard were the kingfishers in the cypress, and the cage of crickets sitting in the sun on the hood of the Pontiac. Miss Mack liked the sound, and said they chirped louder when they were hot.

At noontime, Miss Mack rowed over to the little cemetery. There among the Gavin graves, the two women ate sandwiches and drank Coca-Cola, though Janice, deliberately to antagonize her friend, sometimes insisted on Dr. Pepper instead. Over this lapse of taste, Miss Mack and Janice passed the time in pleasant and practiced argument. In the heat of the afternoon, they returned to the trailer. While Janice napped, Miss Mack sat in the Pontiac—hot though the vinyl seats were—and listened to the baseball game over the radio. This weekly indulgence necessitated always carrying an extra battery in the trunk against the possibility of failure. In the late afternoon, they sat out in folding chairs by the pondside, talking, talking, talking and slapping at mosquitoes. Miss Mack had a large stick across her lap. Every time Janice screamed and pointed out a snake, Miss Mack leaped from her chair and killed the creature with a single blow. She lifted its mangled body on the stick and waved it before Janice's face in retaliation for the Dr. Pepper.

Once Miss Mack killed a rattlesnake in the same manner, hesitating not a single moment in running up to the creature and cudgeling it as ferociously as she would have attacked the most harmless king snake. She sliced off its head and rattles, skinned it, cut out its single line of entrails, and then coiled it up in a buttered skillet and cooked it. She made Janice swallow two bites, and she ate almost all the rest herself.

But most evenings they ate the fish they had caught that day, Miss Mack consuming far more than Janice. After supper they played more cards, or read each other riddles out of paperback books, or just talked, talked, talked.

They drove back to Babylon on Sunday afternoon, arriving sometime after dark, tanned and weary, but already looking forward to the next weekend.

Mr. Hill knew of these trips, and Mr. Hill didn't like them one little bit. Through her friendship with Miss Mack, Janice had changed, and—so far as Mr. Hill was concerned—not for the better. Janice no longer wanted to go to Milton for pizza, because Miss Mack didn't like pizza and Janice had decided that she didn't like it either. Janice no longer considered it a wonderful privilege to be asked to go to Pensacola to a movie, because it was so much more fun to go to the airport and watch the planes take off and land, and try to guess which relatives waiting in the coffee shop would go with which passengers coming through the gate. Mr. Hill didn't even get to see Janice in church on Sunday morning, and sit next to her, and hold her hymnbook, because on Sunday morning Janice was fishing out at Gavin Pond with Miss Mack, getting burned by the sun and eaten up by mosquitoes. Mr. Hill, in short, was worried. He feared that, because of Miss Mack's influence, Janice would refuse his offer of marriage. Mr. Hill's mother, to whom he confessed his anxiety, said, "Miss Mack will never let Janice go. You got to take back what's rightfully yours. And if you cain't think of anything, then you come on back to me, and I'll *tell* you what to do." Quite beyond any consideration of his fondness for Janice Faulk, Mr. Hill had no intention of allowing his comfortable plans to be thwarted by a fat woman with greasy black hair and a face like a pig's.

One day in August, right after a meeting of the teachers preparatory to the beginning of the academic year, Mr. Hill said to Miss Mack, "You gone keep going out to your fishing pond after school starts, Miss Mack?"

"I sure do hope so," replied Miss Mack. "Even though we probably cain't get away until Saturday morning from now on."

Deftly ignoring Miss Mack's *we*, Mr. Hill went on, "Where is that place anyway?"

"It's about ten miles south of DeFuniak Springs."

"Hey you know what? My mama lives in Sweet Gum Head—you know where that is? I have to go through DeFuniak Springs to get there. One of these days when I go visit my mama, I'm gone stop by your place and pay you a visit."

"I wish you would, Mr. Hill. We have got an extra pole, and an extra folding chair. This weekend I'm gone put your name on 'em, and Janice and I will start waiting for you." Under normal circumstances Miss Mack's hospitality would have been extended to Mr. Hill's mother, but in her travels through the Southern countryside, Miss Mack had heard stories about *that* old woman.

Though Janice and Miss Mack returned to Gavin Pond every weekend in September and October, Mr. Hill didn't come to visit them there. Finally one day, toward the end of October, Janice said to Mr. Hill, "Mr. Hill, I thought you were gone go see your mama sometime and stop by and see Miss Mack and me out at the pond. I wish you had, 'cause now it's starting to get cold, and it's not as nice. We're going out this Halloween weekend, but that's gone have to be the last time until spring."

"Oh lord!" cried Mr. Hill, evidently in some perturbation. "Didn't I tell you, Janice?"

"Tell me what?"

"You're gone be needed here at the school for Halloween night."

"Saturday?"

"That's right. I was gone get Miz Flurnoy to do it, but her husband's getting operated on in Pensacola on Friday, and she says she cain't. Gallstones."

Janice was distraught, for she had intended to savor this last weekend at the pond. She came to Miss Mack with a downcast countenance, and told her friend the news.

"Oh, that's not so bad," said Miss Mack. "Tell you what, we just won't go out at all until Sunday. We'll make just the one day of it."

"No sir!" cried Janice. "I don't want you to miss your weekend on my account. You were going out there long before you knew me, and I certainly don't want you to miss your final Saturday out there. Sunday's never as good as Saturday out at the pond, Miss Mack—you know that! You go on, and I'll drive out on Sunday morning. I'll be there before you get up out of the bed!"

Early on Halloween morning, Janice appeared at Miss Mack's door with a paper bag filled with sandwiches. When she answered the bell, Miss Mack fell back from the doorway in apparent alarm. Janice was wearing a Frankenstein mask.

"Is that you under there, Janice? 'Cause if it isn't, I'm sorry, Whoever-you-are, but I don't have a piece of candy in the house. I ate it all up last night!"

Janice removed the mask. "It's me, that's all!" She handed Miss Mack the bag of sandwiches. "I sure do wish I were going too," she sighed.

"You come tomorrow," replied Miss Mack, "and you bring me some Halloween candy. I sure do love Snickers, and they go great with Coca-Cola."

Miss Mack drove off alone in her purple Pontiac, and Janice went to the school cafeteria to begin decorating for the children's Halloween party that night.

At Gavin Pond, Miss Mack altered her routine not one bit, though she admitted to herself, sitting alone in the little green boat in the middle of the pond, that she wished Mr. Hill had chosen somebody else to help with the Halloween party that night. She sorely missed Janice's company. Without her friend, Gavin Pond seemed to Miss Mack a different place altogether.

Just when Miss Mack was thinking that thought for the two hundredth time, she was startled by the sound of an automobile driving along the track that went all the way around the pond. Miss Mack looked up, but could not see the car through the screen of trees. She rowed to shore, hoping very much that it was Janice come to join her after all.

It was not. It was Mr. Hill.

"I had to pick up some things from my mama last evening," said Mr. Hill in explanation, "and I thought I'd stop by on the way back home."

"How'd you find us? This place is about two hundred miles from nowhere!"

"Us?"

"Just me," said Miss Mack. "I'm just so used to Janice being out here, that I said *us* by mistake."

"Too bad she couldn't come," remarked Mr. Hill. "Well, it was Mama who drew me a map."

"Your mama! How'd she know about this place? Gavin Pond's so little and so out-of-the-way they don't even put it on the county maps."

"Oh, Mama's lived around here all her life. My mama knows every square foot of this county," replied Mr. Hill with some pride. "And my mama said to tell you hi, Miss Mack."

"Your mama don't know me from Jezebel's baby sister, Mr. Hill!" exclaimed Miss Mack in a surprise unpleasantly alloyed with a sense—somehow—of having been spied upon.

"My mama," said Mr. Hill, "has heard about you, Miss Mack. My mama is old, but she is interested in many things."

"I had heard that," said Miss Mack uneasily. Miss Mack had also heard that the things that Mrs. Hill interested herself in withered up and died. But Miss Mack did not say that aloud to Mr. Hill, because Mr. Hill evidently loved his mama. He visited her often enough, and was wont to say, in the teachers' lounge, that he always took her advice, and when he didn't take her advice, he should have. Miss Mack just hoped that Mrs. Hill hadn't given her son any advice on the subject of herself and Janice Faulk. Miss Mack liked Mr. Hill well enough, but she knew jealousy when she saw it—in man or woman.

Miss Mack cooked some bream for Mr. Hill's lunch, and they sat and talked for a while in the folding chairs. Miss Mack said how sorry she was that the ball season was over.

About four o'clock Mr. Hill gathered himself up to go. "It sure has been pleasant, Miss Mack. Now I know why you and Janice come out here every single weekend. I'm just real jealous."

"We are pretty happy out here," returned Miss Mack modestly.

"Hey, you know what? It's Halloween. Aren't you gone be scared, being out here all by yourself?"

Miss Mack laughed. "Janice came over this morning wearing a Frankenstein mask, and that didn't scare me one little bit. I've stayed out here all by myself lots and lots of times. Before I knew Janice, I was out here all the time by myself. You don't have to worry about me."

"I'm glad to hear it. Listen, I got to get on back and help out Janice at the school."

"You go on, then. You give her my best, and tell her not to forget my Snickers."

Miss Mack went inside the trailer as Mr. Hill drove off. She was clattering with the pans, or she would have been able to hear that not very far from the trailer, Mr. Hill stopped his car.

In the pine forest it was almost dark. Mr. Hill had just turned onto the track that would lead him back to the dirt road to DeFuniak Springs. He killed the ignition, got out quietly, and opened the trunk. He took out a small corrugated box filled with heavy black ashes mixed with cinders. The rank odor and the lumpish consistency of the blackened remains suggested not the sweeping-out of a coal-burning fireplace, nor a shovelful of some ash heap, but rather something organic, recently dead or even still living, which had been burned, and burned with difficulty.

With a measuring cup that he took from a paper bag in the trunk, Mr. Hill scooped out a portion of the cinders and the ashes, and sprinkled them in one of the ruts of the track that led away from the pond and toward the road. Then he poured a cupful into the other rut, and so alternated until he had distributed the ashes and cinders evenly. Then he tossed the measuring cup and the cardboard box back into the trunk of the car and shut it. Taking then a piece of yellow notepaper from his shirt pocket, he unfolded it, held it close to his eyes in the decreasing light, and in a low voice read the words that had been written upon it. From the same pocket he took a single calendar page—October of the current year—and set fire to it with his cigarette lighter. After this was burned, and the ashes scattered on the ground, Mr. Hill pulled from his trousers a child's compass and a cheap wristwatch—such items as are won in ring-toss booths at traveling carnivals. He checked that the compass needle did indeed point north. He put the wristwatch to his ear to hear its ticking. He dropped both into the heaps of ashes, and crushed them beneath the heel of his shoe.

As Mr. Hill got quietly into his car and drove slowly away, the twilight was deepening into night. The piles of ashes began to blow away. The heavier cinders alone remained, dull and black and moist. The broken springs and face and glass of the wristwatch and compass gleamed only faintly. At a little distance, Miss Mack's crickets in their rabbit cage produced one loud, unison chirp.

Miss Mack fixed more fish for supper. Afterward she cleaned up, and settled down to work a couple of crossword puzzles at the table, but soon gave this over. She had much rather be playing cards with Janice, or trying to guess the riddles that Janice put to her. She went outside, and looked up at the sky. She wore a sweater because the nights were chilly in October. There was a new moon, but the sky was so clear and so bright with stars that Miss Mack had no difficulty in discerning its circle of blackness against the black sky.

She went back inside and went to bed earlier than was usual with her. She was lonely and told herself that the sooner she got to bed, the sooner she might rise. She intended to get up very early, in expectation of Janice's arrival.

Miss Mack awoke at six, or at least at what her internal clock told her was six o'clock. But it obviously wasn't, for the night remained very black. Miss Mack could see nothing at all. She rose and went to the door of the trailer and peered blearily out. It was still deep night, and when she looked toward the east—directly above the little plot of Gavin graves on the far side of the pond—she could discern no lightening of the sky. Miss Mack thought that she had merely been so excited by the prospect of Janice's arrival that she had risen an hour or so before her time. She was about to turn back into the bed for another while, when she suddenly noticed, in the sky, the same black circle of moon as she had seen before.

It hadn't moved.

Miss Mack was confused by this. The moon rose. The moon set. It never stayed still. Perhaps, she attempted to tell herself, it had moved a little. In that case, she had been asleep not eight hours but perhaps only one. That would also explain why it was still so dark. Yet she felt as if she had slept for six or seven hours at the very least.

Miss Mack went back into the trailer and lay down again. If she had slept for only an hour, then she ought to go back to sleep until morning. Perhaps she would be waked by the horn of Janice's car.

But Miss Mack couldn't go back to sleep. She wasn't tired now. She was hungry. She wanted breakfast. So, thinking how foolish she was, she lighted a lamp, and set up the little stove, and cooked bacon and eggs and ate them all up. She stood once more in the doorway of the trailer, and looked out across the pond.

The sky was no lighter. The moon had not moved.

Miss Mack said aloud, "I am dreaming. I am asleep in the bed, and I am having a dream."

She looked at the bed behind her, as if she thought she might indeed see her sleeping self there. She looked back out at the night. She pinched her arm, and held it next to the lamp, watching the flesh turn color.

Nervously, she opened a Coca-Cola, and pulling a sweater over her nightdress, walked out to her car, got in, and turned on the radio. There were only two stations on the air, so she knew it *was* very late at night. More stations came on at four or five with the farm reports. So it had to be earlier than that. She went to WBAM in Montgomery, and got the announcer.

Halloween night—don't let the goblins get you! Lock your doors and close the curtains, boys and girls! It's 2 a.m. and don't walk past any graveyards. This next song goes out to Tommy and Julie, it's . . .

Miss Mack turned the radio off. She was relieved in the main, for at least she knew the time. But still she was puzzled by the moon. She looked up at it, and for a second, was joyed to see that at last it had altered its position. Waking up in the middle of the night always leaves you in a confused state of mind, and she had only made matters worse by eating breakfast at one-thirty in the morning. Sighing, and trusting that *now* she would surely be able to sleep, Miss Mack got out of the Pontiac and slammed the door shut with a grateful bang. She smiled up at the moon—and all her relief washed suddenly away. The *moon* hadn't moved, only *she* had. When she went back to the door of the trailer, and looked again, it still hung the same distance above the top of the same cypress as before she had prepared her untimely breakfast.

Miss Mack returned to the trailer and lay down a third time. Her nervousness she carefully ascribed to the strangeness of being up and about so late at night. She willed herself to sleep, slipped into unconsciousness, and woke at a time that seemed at least several hours later. Certainly she suffered the grogginess and physical lassitude attendant upon too much sleep. She went hastily to the door of the trailer.

The moon had not moved.

This time neglecting her sweater, she ran to the car and turned on the radio. WBAM was playing music, and she turned to the only other station. She heard the end of a song, and then the announcer came on.

And here's the 2 a.m. wrap-up of some of the day's top stories . . .

She turned the radio off.

She sat very still in the front seat of the car, with her chin immobile upon the steering wheel, staring up at the moon, attempting to trace even the slightest movement. She could see none at all.

Miss Mack, with nothing else to do, fixed more bacon and eggs. As she cooked, and as she sat at the table and ate, she refrained from looking out the door at the moon. She saved that for when she had carefully cleaned up. She went with conscious bravery to the door of the trailer and looked out, taking great care to stand exactly where she had stood before so that any slightest alteration of position would be detectable.

The moon had not moved.

It was still 2 A.M. on WBAM, and on the other station as well. This time she listened to the song that was dedicated to Tommy and Julie, and then turned to the wrap-up of some of the day's top stories.

Not much happened on Halloween.

With sudden resolution, Miss Mack ran back to the trailer, quickly dressed, and came back out to the car. She started it up, and backed onto the track. The crickets were in their cage on the backseat, and they brought the voice of the forest along with them. Miss Mack would return to Babylon, and tell Janice that it hadn't been any fun at all, alone on Gavin Pond.

The lights of the car were a little dim—that came from playing the radio so much, and running down the battery. She no longer kept a spare in the car, because ball season was over, and there hadn't been any need for the extra security.

Miss Mack's relief was so great, just to think that she was getting away from Gavin Pond, that she did not realize that she had missed the turnoff until she found herself passing the graveyard on the far side of the pond.

Don't walk past any graveyards.

Miss Mack sped up. In another minute or two she had gone all the way around the pond and was passing by the trailer again. The turnoff was only twenty yards or so beyond the clearing. She put the lights on bright, and slowed considerably.

Before she found the turnoff, the headlights were glancing off the Gavin tombstones. She had missed it again.

Miss Mack went around the pond seven times, looking for the turnoff, and she missed it every time.

That was not possible. She had never once overlooked it before. It was a perfectly obvious break in the trees. The car lights at night would glance off the silicate pebbles in the ruts.

The car lights were growing dimmer with each succeeding turn around the pond. She could tell this by the amount of light that was reflected off the tombstones. The moon didn't move. The chirping of the crickets in the backseat grew clamorous. Miss Mack threw the car into park suddenly, reached over into the back, and flung the cage out the window.

It hit the trunk of a tree, and must have broken open, for the chirping dispersed. Miss Mack immediately regretted her action. Having given Mr. Hill all the fish she had caught the previous day, having consumed all her bacon and eggs in the course of the two nervous breakfasts, she had now nothing to eat. And she had just disposed of the bait she might have used to catch more fish. It was little comfort to remember that fish didn't bite at night.

Miss Mack drove around more slowly now, and even began to look for the track leading to the DeFuniak Springs road on the opposite side of the pond from where she knew it to be. She pinched her fat arms until they were bruised and raw, hoping with each attack to wake up in any place but this.

Miss Mack realized suddenly that not only was she wearing down her battery, she was using up her gas. She had very little left. She hadn't looked at the odometer when she first attempted to drive away from Gavin Pond—why should she have?—but she suspected that she had already driven thirty-five or forty miles. On a straight road, that would have carried her all the way back to Babylon.

The moon hadn't moved.

Miss Mack stopped the car by the trailer, got out, and went inside. She sat down exhausted on the bed. She went to sleep again, and slept for she knew not how long. She hoped that when she waked it would be day, that Janice would wake her by knocking on the door of the trailer. She hoped all this had been a dream —it certainly had the qualities of a dream—and that she might precipitate its ending by rendering herself unconscious within its confines.

She waked, and it was night. Without daring to look at the moon, she went back out to the car. It started, but sluggishly. WBAM was still dedicating a song to Tommy and Julie, and she had very nearly memorized the 2 A.M. wrap-up. Miss Mack drove around and around the pond, and the Pontiac's wavering headlights fell in brutal alternation, now upon the metal trailer, now upon the white Gavin tombstones. She was no longer even looking for the turnoff. She drove as fast as she could around and around the pond, until the car, out of gas, rolled to a standstill just beyond the graveyard.

Miss Mack tried the radio one more time.

Faintly came the song for Tommy and Julie. She listened to it all the way through, thinking, If he plays another song, then I'll *know* that time is passing, and I'll be all right. If he starts over again, then I'll *know* that I'm dreaming.

The battery failed on the last notes of Tommy and Julie's song.

The car lights, which she had left on, faded to blackness.

Miss Mack got out, and turned back. She walked past the graveyard, and slowly along the track from which the turnoff had unaccountably and indisputably disappeared. All the way back to the trailer, she stared at the ruts in the earth, and kept her mind solely upon the turnoff—she did not wish to miss it in her distraction. But the turnoff was not there. She did not stop at the trailer, but continued around again, until she came to the Pontiac, still ticking away its heat.

Don't walk past any graveyards.

From this point, it seemed useless to keep on in the track. She struck out into the pine forest, heading directly north, to where the dirt road led up to DeFuniak Springs. Her way and her speed were impeded by tangled undergrowth and briers. The forest and the night were so dark that she sometimes walked directly into trees, not having been able to see them. Yet swiftness was not of such concern as was the maintenance of her direction. She forged straight ahead, knowing that if she only walked far enough, she would get *some*where.

She had lost sight of the darkened moon, for the canopy of tree limbs was too thick to permit her to see it. But it was behind her, she knew, and she took some comfort with the reflection that she was walking away from it. At last, after she had walked about an hour, Miss Mack came to a little clearing in the forest. She caught a glimpse of dark water—but even before she had seen the trailer and the gleaming tombstones on the far side, she realized that she had returned to Gavin Pond.

She made another attempt, and struck out directly southward. There was a farm road probably no more than a mile distant, with some old tenant-farmer shacks on it. Miss Mack no longer cared whether they were inhabited or not. If only she could reach that road she would be safe.

She walked for a time she knew not how to measure. It might have been for thirty minutes, or it might have been for hours. And even more carefully than before, she maintained her direction—of that she was certain.

Yet once again, she came upon the clearing in the forest, the trailer, the glint of tombstones on the other side of the water.

For the first time in her life, Miss Mack felt real and uncontrollable fear. By no means could she get away from Gavin Pond. There was no turnoff from the circular track. All ways out through the forest led directly back to the clearing. She had no food in the cabin, and no bait with which to fish. Her lamp oil would not last forever, and tomorrow morning would never come. Miss Mack's one hope was that she was asleep and dreaming. With this single thought, Miss Mack went inside the trailer, lay down upon the bed, and went to sleep. When she waked, it was night—still Halloween night. The moon hadn't moved.

Introduction:

Hollow Eyes

BY GUY N. SMITH

Guy N. Smith lives on a picturesque farm in the misty hills of Shropshire, within sight of the Welsh border, where he and his family are almost entirely self-sufficient, even growing their own tobacco and making their own elderberry wine. When he comes in from the fields, he writes novels, turning out three or four each year. Their titles, which adequately speak for themselves, read like a *What's What* of horror; among them are *Bats Out of Hell, Killer Crabs, Crabs on the Rampage, Son of the Werewolf, Wolfcurse, The Ghoul, The Slime Beast,* and *The Sucking Pit.*

"Hollow Eyes," one of his rare short stories, is an example of the style that's uniquely his own.

Hollow Eyes

BY GUY N. SMITH

For a few seconds everything stopped for Lester Miles. Around him this world of seasonal make-believe ceased to exist, the garish rubber and plastic masks of the noisy revellers faded, shadows and silence surging out of the background to make him a man alone. Blackness spotted with red spared him temporarily the vision of that awful thing dangling from the bough of the tree. Gut-churning shock merged into a numbness that was both physical and mental. Every muscle in his body was petrified, his brain a sluggish computer that said ease up, start from the beginning again and maybe everything will change and that gaudy bobbing orb will turn out to be just another pumpkin on Halloween night.

It won't!

Try it and see. You don't have any choice.

Okay then, let's go back to the beginning.

He sensed rather than saw the shadowy shapes gathered in a half-circle watching him through the eye-slits in their bogey masks, felt the vibrations of their whispers in the still atmosphere but did not hear their voices. Kids, teenagers some of them, doing what every kid did on Halloween, trick-or-treating. *Tell us a tale, mister, and make it spooky, 'cause we're all spooks tonight. You, too.*

Lester closed his eyes, felt the thumping of his heart, heard a roaring in his ears that might have been that big bonfire across the park just lit, the hungry flames eating up the piles of tinder-dry brushwood. He fingered the loaded .38 in the pocket of his windcheater and remembered again why he was here. Julie, his sixteen-year-old daughter, was somewhere amongst this way-out crowd; Hutch, too. The thought of Hutch had his finger tightening on the trigger, and if the safety had not been on, it would have blasted a hole in his pocket, maybe killed someone. And he wasn't going back home to face Lucy until he'd killed Hutch because it was the only way.

Hutch was a slob, the kind you found in most city subways after ten at night, sleeping rough, rotting his life away. A pity he had not gone the way of most of his kind a long time ago. The drugs gave them brief hope, then killed them, only somehow Hutch had survived. Because he was more cunning than the rest. Find yourself a rich man's daughter, and milk her and her folks for everything they've got. Either that or rot in the gutter.

So Hutch had found himself Julie. Jesus, Lester could not understand what she saw in that dropout. Overweight and dirty so that you involuntarily caught your breath if he got too close to you, a belly that rolled out of the waistline of his tattered jeans, a walk like a duck with a sprained leg. A beard grown out of laziness and an attempt to cover up those patches of acne except that the hair had failed to germinate in places and gave the impression of a disfiguration of the skin, that harelip a permanent sneer. I've got your daughter, rich man, and I'm screwing her. Don't waste your time trying to stop me because that way you'll just lose your little girl.

You've lost her.

No! That isn't . . .

Just tell us a spooky story. Start right from the beginning and don't miss anything out.

Hutch had taken to coming to the house most nights this last month, biding his time until Julie came in from the office. He would have been back in the gutters where he belonged if Lucy hadn't held her husband back. "Don't, Lester, it won't do any good. At least we know where Julie is if Hutch comes here. Maybe she'll get tired of him, find somebody else. Let it blow itself out naturally. And don't be too hard on the boy, because if he goes, Julie might go with him. Promise me that, Lester."

Lester had promised, and broken that promise three nights later. Tonight. Halloween night.

Lucy had gone downtown to her mother's as she always did on Friday evenings, a routine which they had got into since her mother came out of hospital almost a year ago. Lester usually returned home from his office about six and if his wife hadn't put him a cold supper in the fridge then Julie cooked him something.

Christ, he didn't have any appetite those times when Hutch was there, that fat stinking youth sitting up the corner swigging beer out of a can and belching. I'm screwing your daughter, rich man, so don't try to stop me drinking your beer. There's plenty more where this came from. Get me?

Only tonight Lester Miles had arrived home an hour earlier than usual. The streets were going to be bedlam with trick-or-treating and he just wanted to lock himself in his own house until it was all over, turn up the TV, and ignore the doorbell.

Hutch and Julie were going to the Halloween Fair in the park. That much was obvious when Lester let himself in, saw the colourful costumes draped over the chair in the hall, a werewolf mask grinning at him with bloodied fangs. He's screwing your daughter, rich man. Run for the stairs and see for yourself. Hurry, they're sure to be listening out for you.

Lester ran, took the stairs three at a time, kicked open the door of Julie's room like a gunfighter in a B Western movie. He pulled up, wanted to look away and when he looked back again everything would be all right and they wouldn't be here after all. Just a trick of the brain. Trick-or-treat. Jesus H. Christ!

Hutch was even fatter than you thought when you saw him with his clothes off, a bulbous pink spotty thing that would have been funny any other place except here. Julie, grabbing for him as he rolled off her because she was so close she had to finish even if her old man was watching.

If the .38 had been handy Lester would have shot them both, maybe turned the snub-nosed barrel on himself afterwards. But the pistol was downstairs in a locked drawer of his desk and somehow his reactions had slowed up, enough so that Hutch was pushing him out of the way, dragging Julie naked down the stairs after him.

And when Lester finally made it down to the hallway those costumes and masks were gone, so he knew that they had gone to the park after all. That was when he went into the room he used as an office, unlocked the bottom drawer of the desk, and groped under a pile of receipted bills until he found the gun. He knew then what he had to do, the only way Hutch could be stopped. Oh Jesus God!

They were still watching him, that silent arc of shadowy shapes with their gruesome masks that suddenly weren't colourful anymore. Whispering in unison. *Tell us a tale, mister, and make it a spooky one. Maybe that way it will turn out all right after all.* And that thing dangling from the bough will be just a pumpkin after all.

Lester Miles kept his eyes tightly shut because he didn't want to know what it was, let his mind go back an hour or so. He had called in at the chemist's on the corner and bought himself a mask, a grinning ghoul with scarlet blood trickling out of the stretched mouth and a fringe of hair on the top that tickled his own receding hairline. It was the only way he was going to be able to move freely in the park and he didn't want Hutch to recognise him until he got real close. He'd identify Hutch, all right, nothing could disguise that misshapen, slouching form. No mask or costume could protect the bastard who was screwing Lester's daughter.

The park resembled some weird rock festival, screaming hordes of pseudo-demons coming at you, shrieking and wheeling, screams of mock terror. Lester was sweating beneath his mask; it was too small, made for a ten-year-old, but it would do. The atmosphere was hazy, maybe later on the mist would roll in. He shivered at the thought. God, this was one festival that ought to be banned. Muggers took advantage of it, wore their disguises openly tonight, for no patrolling policeman would stop and check. The forces of evil were given the freedom of the city for just one night every year.

The kids had built the usual mountainous bonfire in the same place where they built it every year, a fifteen-foot-high pile of broken furniture and every conceivable item of rubbish that the surrounding neighbourhood had been saving up for tonight. On the summit there was some kind of effigy, the usual figure made from discarded clothing stuffed with newspapers. It was barbaric, an old pagan rite in which a person was burned alive to appease the old gods. Tonight civilisation went right back to its roots.

Lester hurried on, had to turn his head from side to side in order to see the cavorting silhouettes all around him. Kids and teenagers, little ones, big ones; thin ones, fat ones—but none yet as gross as Hutch. But the night was young and he would find him. There was murder in his heart but tonight that was all right.

The park was big, too big. In places the street lighting barely reached but he could still make out the figures as he passed them. He would not overlook the one he sought.

Something bobbed in front of him, twisted on a length of plastic string from the branch a couple of feet above, spun one way, then the other. Now you see it, now you don't. A pumpkin or turnip lantern; he would have passed it by except that there was something odd about it, something which halted his fast stride and had him peering closer. The orange light was just bright enough for him to make out the thick waxen features and still it wasn't quite right. He stepped closer, felt his stomach heave up as the thing swung back to face him.

The eyes should have been crude holes, the nose a triangular shape, the mouth an oblong slit. Instead the features were just too realistic, finely moulded beneath a layer of smeared wax, lips pouted cheekily as though glued into a pert posture. Hollow eyes as if the orbs had been gouged out of their living sockets, yet those cavities still saw . . . and *understood.* Yet the face was in darkness, no candle burning within, casting its flickering light like some mocking mischievous demon. Just too real and in the end Lester Miles accepted the fact that it *was* real; recognised those features and recoiled beneath the cold stare from those hollow eyes.

You've found me but it's too late. Too late!

The bile came up and scorched his throat. He tried to jerk his gaze away but it would not move. The head swung away, came tantalisingly back at him again, a momentum akin to the pendulum of a grandfather clock. Now you see me again. Look closely, just to make sure.

He thought he screamed *"Julie!"* a shriek that echoed in his brain, had his vision reeling, blurring into a kaleidoscope that eventually turned black with tinges of red. The background noise had ceased, the orange glow dimmed. Just those shadowy watching shapes. *Tell us a story, mister, and make it a spooky one. Maybe that way everything will be all right after all.*

No, it won't. That's my Julie's head bobbing there, killed by that bastard Hutch. You don't have your daughter anymore, rich man. Go tell your wife. Didn't she say to leave me alone, let me screw your daughter? Now *you've* killed her because you wouldn't listen.

Slowly Miles emerged from the hypnotism of those hollow eyes, found he did not have to look at them any longer.

The orange glow was back and the silent watchers were gone to join their colleagues away towards the big fire. He could hear their shouts, their laughter, voices in unison calling for the bonfire to be lighted. They had gone and left him alone with his daughter.

He found that he could move again, turned, and began to retrace his steps. That roaring was still inside his head but now it seemed to have a purpose, a kind of inbuilt turbo-engine driving him on. A man with one purpose left in life. Revenge. He had to find Hutch before the darkness of Halloween Night swallowed him up, took him back into its bosom of evil.

Lester Miles walked fast, soon caught up with the milling throng. Hundreds of kids were wailing for the fire to be lit in the same way that they might have done a thousand years ago. Burn the sacrifice; do not keep the gods waiting.

God, it was crazy. These were no ordinary fun-loving kids, not the kind you found at an ordinary bonfire party. There was something vicious about them, gremlins unleashed upon a city, given human shape and masks to hide their gargoyle-like features. Their cries were frenzied now, a single word, a demand, repeated over and over again.

"Burn . . . burn . . . burn . . ."

Hutch had to be here somewhere. Miles jostled with the crowd, felt his skin crawl as he made contact with them. Bodies that felt chilled, colder than the atmosphere of a fall evening. Like living corpses.

He tried to get himself under control. He was distraught, his imagination was playing tricks on him. Tricking and treating. *Tell us a story, mister, and make it a spooky one.* Okay, it's a deal, find me Hutch and I'll give you a real spooky yarn.

Lester heard the flames crackling, smelled the acrid stench of woodsmoke. Suddenly the whole scene was lighted up so brightly that it had him closing his eyes again. I don't want to see anything except Hutch; this is hell with its own demons roasting in the fires.

He found himself stepping back, moving away from the scorching heat. Sparks showered up into the night sky, burning debris floating down, and that figure on the top of the pile, shifting as though it had already begun to writhe in agony, was screaming its terror of the leaping flames.

Lester's features hardened behind his claustrophobic mask; that was what he would like to do to Hutch: burn the bastard. Roast him, watch the flesh melt off his bones until there was only a skeleton left and . . .

A jangling noise interrupted his sadistic thoughts. Some kids were hustling him, shaking a tin bucket with a handful of pennies in the bottom. Trick-or-treat.

"I . . . uh . . ." He felt a fleeting sense of embarrassment as he fumbled in his pocket for some loose change, felt the cold hardness of the .38. Leering artificial faces seemed to take on an extra dimension of evil in the dancing light from the flames. He spilled some of the coins and the children were stooping, scrabbling for them in the grass. "Any of you kids seen a fat guy called . . ."

Lester's muffled words came back at him. They did not hear, weren't listening. They wouldn't have told him even if they had seen Hutch; they would protect their own kind.

Alone again, standing back from the crowd. His anger simmered and for a few moments he was a law-abiding citizen again. It was wrong taking the law into his own hands like this. Foolish. This was a police matter. Officer, I wish to report a first-degree killing. Ronald Arthur Hutchinson, of no fixed abode, has murdered my daughter. Decapitated her, suspended her head from . . . ugh! The bile burned his throat again . . . from a branch of a tree. He's somewhere here, amongst this crowd of vicious kids. They're all the same, they'd kill me, you too. Tonight's the night when evil reigns supreme, unchecked.

May I have your name and address, sir? And a description of the suspect. We'll do our best to apprehend him. But it may take time. There's hundreds of kids in the park and they all look alike. And I don't think they're *all* bad, sir.

They're all bloody rotten to the core, Officer. Just look at them. They're carrying knives openly, and Christ knows what other weapons they've got hidden under their costumes. They're all killers looking for somebody to kill. Possessed. And I'm possessed, too.

The evil flooded back into Lester Miles. He felt his pulses throbbing, the overwhelming desire to take human life; Hutch's, but he would kill others too. Tonight sacrifices were demanded, the old ones were getting impatient. Sod the law, *he* was the law. He fingered the .38 again, slipped the safety on and off again. Hutch first, after that it didn't matter. Just kill.

He moved back closer to the fire, winced at the heat. Cavorting shapes everywhere, wailing voices like a fleet of police sirens. But the police would not come here tonight, they knew only too well when to keep away.

Then he became aware of the stench. It rasped into his nostrils through the nose holes in the mask, filtered down into his throat and brought on a fit of coughing, shaking his whole body. He tried to identify the odour; bitter, not just old tyres and smouldering upholstery but something which was vaguely familiar. Like over-roasting meat . . . He recalled that time a few weeks ago when Lucy had forgotten the pork chops in the oven. They had burned to a cinder, smoke billowing out and filling the kitchen so that they had had to open all the windows. It had taken days to get the stink out of the kitchen. It was like that now only much stronger, much worse. He retched and a movement, a shifting on top of the blaze, caught his eye.

Lester Miles froze into immobility for the second time that night. Again his brain refused to accept what his eyes saw in that blinding orange light. The heat was so intense that everybody else had backed off, leaving him alone once more, a ring of shapes beyond the circle of firelight, the wails dying down to rustling sinister whispers. *Tell us a story, mister, and make it a spooky one. After that everything will be all right.*

The effigy had slid, the flames having burned through the ropes which had held it in place. The ragged clothing smouldered and fell away, jeans and denim jacket disintegrating before Lester's eyes. Beneath the garments there should have been balls of crumpled newspapers showering down in an avalanche of fire. But there weren't; the body was firm and blackened, smouldering and giving off that vile stench, overdone meat roasting, the fat melting and dripping just like those pork chops had done in the kitchen back home that day. A human body being consumed by fire, a ghastly sprawled obese shape, the belly flesh hanging in rolls and pouches.

The corpse moved again, threatening to come tumbling down from its funeral pyre, the head twisting and lolling, staring down at the man below and seeming to see him with those dead hollow eyes. Lester saw the expression on that cooked face, the mouth stretched into a hideous grin behind the wisps of smoking beard, heard the voice that came from everywhere, yet nowhere in particular, those guttural tones which he had come to loathe and recognised as belonging to Hutch.

"I didn't kill her, Mr. Miles. God's truth, I didn't. It was *them!* They'll kill you just as they killed me."

Lying bastard, lying right up until the very end! Lester's vision swam and then cleared as his fury came to its peak. He saw again the bobbing severed head, the way Julie's lips pouted cheekily at him, the vile symbol of this night when civilisation retreated and hid. He smelled death and burning human meat and that was when he dragged the .38 from his pocket.

The first bullet missed, sent up a shower of sparks; the second ploughed into the cooking skull, tore the forehead open, a gaping wound that spilled out blobs of congealed blood, gravy for the roast. Firing wildly now, he could hear the slugs slamming into the body. Hutch jerked, started to roll, dead arms splayed as though reaching out to encircle the one who had done this to him. A scream, "I didn't do it, Mr. Miles. *They* did!"

The firing pin was clicking mechanically when the blazing fireball that had once been Hutch landed at Lester's feet, rolled over and stared up at him still grinning. "You got it all wrong, Mr. Miles, but it's too late now."

Lester sensed the shadowy shapes moving in, a shifting circle in which only the gaudily painted bogey masks were visible. Hands clutched him viciously, tore at him, gouged his flesh as they lifted him aloft, held him there. The chant was rising again . . .

"Burn . . . burn . . . burn . . ."

Tell us a tale, mister, and make it a spooky one. Maybe that way everything will be all right . . .

Introduction:

The Halloween House

BY ALAN RYAN

I like Halloween. I like the cool time of year when it comes, and the autumn colors, especially the orange and black that symbolize it in America, suggesting the union of life and death. I like the long and dishonorable history of the holiday, and the rich body of lore it has acquired over the centuries. I like the time-honored ways of marking the occasion, some of which, despite their bloody sources, are—or seem—mere games for children now. I like the fact that this holiday provokes a shiver to go with the smile. I like Halloween because it reminds us of our mortality.

I've written a couple of novels about the town of Deacons Kill. For this Halloween tale, Deacons Kill seemed the right place to go.

The Halloween House

BY ALAN RYAN

Cruel October pinched the cheeks of children and iced the blood of the elderly. The children tumbled from the school bus and laughed at the tingle and sprinted a little faster. The old folks, sitting by windows, waiting for the children to come home, looked at their whitened fingers and pressed their lips together and knew that worse was on its way.

Along the breezy streets of Deacons Kill, windows were closed the final inch, and here and there chimneys began slowly coughing gray smoke. Auto exhausts billowed white. The corners of windows grew misty. The front hallways of houses smelled faintly of closets and camphor as winter coats were taken out and placed where they'd be handy. Shoes scuffed leaves in the street and tires crunched them, and the leaves, startled, whirled like angry birds and settled back nervously to the ground. Any day now. Any minute.

The children went on laughing and running.

The old folks looked again and again at their bloodless fingers, rubbed icy hands together, tugged sweaters closer around bony shoulders, and waited.

Any day now. Any minute.

Dale Martin shivered, then shivered again as he tried to conceal his reaction to the sharp bite of the wind.

But Colleen caught it. "Cold?" she said.

"No," he said quickly. "You?"

He was freezing and afraid that his teeth would start chattering any second now. That would be swell. Just swell. He clenched his teeth together and held his jaw muscles tight and pulled his arms in close against his body. He wished he'd worn more than a light windbreaker to school today.

"A little," Colleen said.

"Do you want to stop for coffee or hot chocolate or something?"

Please, he urged her silently.

She considered the idea for a few steps. She was always doing that, Dale thought, even in the classroom when the teacher asked a question. It was one of the things he liked about her. She wasn't silly like all the other girls. She'd never just answer a question right out; she'd always stop and think first, and when she spoke, she always said exactly what she was thinking. Dale wished he could do the same right now.

"That would be nice," Colleen said. "I could use a cup of coffee."

But Dale could tell from her tone of voice that she was going to say something else. His fingers felt like Popsicles. He shoved his hands deeper into his pockets and kept silent. Strong and silent, that was him. Out of the corner of his eye, he saw her glance sideways at him and wondered if she could tell that he was freezing.

"But there's really something else I'd like to do"—she paused, timed it perfectly, and they both knew it—"if you wouldn't mind."

"Sure," he said.

Anything. As long as it's out of the cold. And as long as it's with you. I'm a junior, he thought. You're a sophomore. I should be doing better than this. It had taken him two whole weeks to set up this casual walk home from school.

"What is it?"

She looked sideways at him, so he had to turn his head and face her. "I want to visit the Grainger place," she said, and her eyes were bright.

"The haunted house?" He couldn't help himself.

"Yes. I've heard about it ever since I moved here. I'd really like to see it, and this is the perfect time."

Dale thought fast. It was at least a fifteen-minute walk to the Grainger house from here. And another fifteen back, plus the rest of the walk home, plus however long they stayed at the Grainger place. He wished he could look at his watch but he didn't have the nerve. And he'd promised his mother he'd absolutely be home on time for dinner tonight, especially because everyone would be in a hurry to get to the Halloween bonfire later; his mother had been raising hell lately, anyway, about being stuck in the kitchen all evening because of him, but he couldn't tell Colleen he had to stop along the way to call his *mother.*

"Please," Colleen said. "It's the perfect time for it."

He loved the way she left it up to him. Well then, he'd just have to make some excuse at home and take the consequences. A man's gotta do what a man's gotta do.

"Sure," he said. "No problem. C'mon, it's up this way."

They turned a corner and a gust of wind instantly snatched at them, making them duck their heads into their collars.

"Thanks, Dale," she said beside him.

"Sure," he said.

"Happy Halloween," she said. She sounded so happy.

"Happy Halloween."

"Look, it's starting to get dark already. Oh, this'll be fun. It'll be great!" She took her hand out of her pocket and, pressing her side against him, linked her arm with his.

He forced a grin with cheeks stiff from the cold.

"Happy Halloween," he said again.

And they started up the long and silent road toward the Grainger place, with branches creaking above their heads and the wind snapping at their faces and brittle shadows pacing them step for step.

"Is that it?" Colleen cried. "That must be it. God, it's creepy!" She clutched dramatically at Dale's arm.

"That's it," said Dale.

They had left the last of both houses and sidewalk some distance back, and had just rounded a sharp bend in the road. A wall of dark green pines had hidden the way ahead, but now they had a perfect view of the old Grainger house. It was still farther up the hillside, on their right, and they'd still have some trekking to do before they actually reached the front door, but they could see it in all its spooky detail from where they stood. If the house, uninhabited for years and years, had actually stood right beside the road, where it could be seen readily from up close, the local people might never have dubbed it "the haunted house." But it was not beside the road, and its distance and inaccessibility—it was at the very top of a sparsely wooded hill, and reachable only by a narrow driveway that curved beneath arching trees—added to its air of decrepit mystery. Now, as Dale and Colleen looked up at it, the house was outlined against the pale light of the overcast sky, and it was everything a haunted house on a hilltop ought to be.

There were great rounded turrets at each corner and a row of jagged-looking gables across the top, surmounted by a cupola. Time had not been kind to the house and, even from this distance, its outlines seemed almost to have been worn and rounded by the ravages of wind and weather. Oddly, there were only two windows at the front in all of the upper floor. The first floor had once been surrounded by what must have been a magnificent porch, but the porch was now in a sorry state of decay, the roof sagging drunkenly where it hadn't actually rotted through and collapsed. It certainly didn't look capable of surviving another winter. Or, for that matter, another windy night. The whole structure, looking as if it were ready to settle sadly back into the earth, was an unhealthy shade of sickly gray.

"I think it's Victorian," Dale said, trying his best to sound casual, knowledgeable, worldly, mature.

"It is," Colleen said. "Architecture is one of my hobbies. That's why I love exploring old houses. Come on! I can't wait to see it up close. Oh, Dale, thank you for bringing me here." She squeezed his hand.

"Sure thing," Dale said. "My pleasure."

Colleen darted ahead and ducked into the overgrown driveway that obviously led up to the house. She quickly got ahead of him, then stopped and turned and, laughing merrily, called, "Come on, slowpoke! Don't leave me here all alone with the goblins!"

Although Dale wasn't certain how or why, this whole thing seemed to be slipping rapidly out of his control. For a single, crazy instant, he wished that Colleen were just a little bit less pretty, her lips less red, her cheeks less pink from the cold. But she was just as pretty as ever—prettier, in fact, now that she was here with him and she was happy—so he produced a smile, told her "Don't worry, I'll protect you!" and trudged up the driveway behind her.

"No, wait," he said, and took hold of her arm. They were standing on the damp earth, amid withering weeds, in front of the first step up to the porch. "Better let me test it first. Those steps don't look like they'll hold much weight."

This October had been rainier than usual, and the wooden steps of the porch, exposed to the worst of the elements here at the top of the hill, seemed to have absorbed more than their share of wetness. The wood, almost entirely bare of paint, was a dark, sad brownish gray, twisted and split in places, and looked as if it might settle at any minute into the soggy earth below and become one with it. Dale was certain that the pressure of a foot would crack right through the wood; more likely, the rotting step would turn to mush beneath the weight.

"Don't come up till I say it's okay," he told Colleen sternly.

"Thank you, Dale," Colleen said.

Dale pondered for an instant the relationship of men and women in this world, then took a deep breath and approached the steps. His shoes made a squishy noise in the dirt.

To get the measure of things, he placed one foot in the middle of the bottom step and applied some pressure. The step sagged at once. It was rotten right through. He moved to the side of the steps and kicked lightly at the wooden support that hid the space beneath them. His shoe made a dull thud against it, but the wood of the upright sounded solid enough. He placed his foot at the end of the bottom step—there was no railing or banister—and leaned forward. The supports swayed ever so slightly but felt sturdy enough to hold his weight.

He went up the steps to the porch, keeping carefully to the outer edge and placing each foot in front of the other. The structure moved a little beneath him, as if its base shifted just a bit in the soggy earth, but it held.

"Ta da!" he cried when he reached the porch. He stayed at the very edge here too, not trusting the rotting wood of the floor to support his weight. He held on to a column beside the steps—its peeling paint, soggy with rain, felt slimy beneath his hand—and turned to Colleen.

"Sir Edmund Hillary!" she said, looking up at him and laughing.

"You bet!" Dale said. He made a mental note to look that one up.

"Come on." He stretched a hand down to her and warned her to stay at the edge of the steps, the way he had. In a second, she was on the porch beside him.

"Stay right here," he told her. "I have to test this floor."

With one hand holding the slippery column, he banged a heel against the floor of the porch. Nothing happened. He banged again, a little harder. This time, his heel punched a shallow indentation into the rotting wood. "No good," he said. "We'll have to stick to the structural supports." He wished he could remember what you call those beams that hold up floors. He spotted the line of rusty nailheads across the warped boards of the porch. "Here," he said. He tested his weight, took one step, staying right on the line of nails, then another. The porch made some weary creaking noises but it held. Now they could get to the door.

"Okay," he said. "We're on our way. One haunted house, coming up. Just let me make sure I can get the door open."

The greenish brass plate seemed ready to pull completely free of the decaying wood, but the knob turned readily enough when he touched it. Almost instantly, the door swung open, making a soft sound, a kind of *plop,* as it came free of the jamb, as if a rubber seal or something of the sort had been holding it in place.

It was only now, with the door actually open before him on the murky interior of the house—he could smell the mustiness of it already—that Dale realized that, all along, he'd been hoping they wouldn't be able to get in.

"Great, it's open," he said.

"Terrific!" Colleen said, and came and stood beside him on the doorsill.

The air inside the house was thick and stale, with a hint of an odd odor that couldn't be readily named. It seemed both unpleasant and strangely familiar, all at the same time. Dale pushed the door all the way back to let in as much fresh air as possible, and the odor dissipated at once. The open door also let in some light, which was welcome, because almost none at all came in through the grimy windows, further obscured as they were by the sagging roof of the porch.

"Great," said Colleen. "Isn't this great?"

"Great," said Dale.

But, actually, it wasn't as bad as it might have been. The dampness seemed not to have penetrated the interior of the house too badly, and when he tested the floor of the entryway with his heel, he found it relatively dry and solid. When he put his full weight on the floor in the middle of the foyer—holding his breath while he did it and wondering if he'd plunge right through the boards up to his neck—it held him perfectly without the slightest shift or creak.

"It's okay," he told Colleen, "we're in. Better leave the door open."

Stealthily now, enjoying it, they advanced a little way into the house. Even with the door wide open, it was still dark inside. Dale was peering through an arched doorway off the foyer that must once have led to a living room or sitting room, when Colleen spotted the stairs. It was a fine-looking staircase, rising up against the wall and bending around a corner just where the darkness enveloped it, and protected by a fancy-looking banister with carved railings and large newel posts.

"I want to go upstairs," Colleen said. "Let's go upstairs first, okay, Dale?"

"I guess," Dale said.

They started up the stairs. Dale insisted on going first, to be sure the staircase was safe at each step.

"This place must have been sealed tighter than a drum," he said over his shoulder when they were halfway up. "The damp doesn't seem to have gotten in at all." He was sliding his right hand along the wall as he went up and it felt as dry as a bone. He tapped it with his knuckles and it sounded perfectly solid. "No decay in here at all."

"You sound like a dentist," Colleen said, and they both giggled.

The second floor hallway was even darker than the foyer. They could barely see a thing, although there was very little, in fact, to see. They could just make out several doorways, one of which was slightly ajar. When Dale pushed it open, they could see that it was one of the front rooms with a single window, though the window admitted hardly any light at all. They pushed open the other doors—they all opened readily enough, with the same *plop* the front door had made—but, with the darkness of the house and the emptiness of the rooms, there was little point in exploring further.

"Do you think we should go downstairs, Dale?" Colleen asked.

"I think so, yeah," Dale said.

When they got downstairs, they discovered that the darkness of the outside world was rapidly growing to match that of the interior of the house. And the dampness of the air, rushing in now through the open front door, made them both shiver. Dale thought the newel post at the bottom of the banister had felt wet to the touch, as if the chilly moisture from outside had condensed there.

"Maybe we should be getting back," Dale said. "It's getting pretty dark out."

Colleen was peeking into the sitting room, but the house was so dark now that it was impossible to see anything.

"I guess you're right," she said, and sighed. "I wish we could see it on a bright day, or with a flashlight. Or, better yet, by candlelight."

"Yeah," said Dale.

They were at the doorway when Colleen took hold of his arm.

"Dale," she said, "do you think we could come back sometime? Do you think we could? I'd be afraid to come by myself."

If they hurried, they'd just be able to make it back to town before the light of day was gone completely.

"Absolutely," Dale said. "Your wish is my command. Be careful there on the porch and the steps."

When they were safely back on the damp ground, Colleen turned to him and smiled her prettiest smile. "Thank you, Dale," she said warmly. "I really mean it. Thanks a lot." And she kissed him with those lovely red lips right on his willing mouth.

As they turned away from the house, his arm snugly around her shoulders and hers snugly around his waist, Dale noticed that he'd left the front door open, but he wasn't about to go back and close it now.

He made it home just in the nick of time. His mother turned from the stove and looked at him significantly, but she didn't complain and only told him to hurry and wash up for dinner, and to leave those muddy shoes by the door.

"What's gotten into you, Dale?" his father said as soon as they were all seated at the dinner table. "You look almost happy, as if you've shaken off the adolescent doldrums for a change."

"Oh, nothing," Dale said, but he grinned pleasantly around the table, and just a bit smugly.

"He's got a girlfriend," said Bethy.

"Mind your own business!" Dale told her.

"I'm eight years old," Bethy said calmly. "That means I'm old enough to speak my mind."

Dale growled, "That means you're old enough to get your little neck bro—"

"That's enough, the two of you," Dale's mother said. "Bethy, don't leave those string beans on your plate. Dale, eat your dinner, you're still a growing boy."

"Yeah," said Bethy, "he'll need all the strength he can get, now that he has a girlfriend."

"Listen—" Dale began.

"Cut it out," his father said. "Everybody cut it out and just eat."

Every now and then through the meal, Bethy hummed "Dale's got a girlfriend," and Dale glowered at her across the table, but nothing further was said on the subject.

Dale finished ahead of the others and said, very casually, "You guys mind if I go ahead to the bonfire?"

"We are not 'you guys,' " his father said wearily.

"Dale," his mother said, "you haven't even asked your sister if she had a good time trick-or-treating."

"Did you have a good time trick-or-treating?"

"Yes," Bethy said sweetly. "I got all sorts of good stuff. Except I didn't get a girlfriend, like you did."

"You know, Mom," Dale said, "we may have to get that child replaced. I think it's defective."

His father sighed. "Dale," he said, "why don't you go ahead to the bonfire and us guys will meet you there, okay?"

"Hey, terrific idea, Dad! See you later." He was away from the table in a flash.

"Wear something warm," his mother called after him.

"And don't get into trouble," his father said.

"Yeah, don't get into trouble," Bethy echoed as he was going out the door.

Deacons Kill had a giant bonfire every year on Halloween and no one in town would have thought of missing it. The materials for the fire—old broken pieces of furniture as well as cordwood—were all stacked in place. The ground was already cleared, and portable fire extinguishers were in readiness. The people of the town had begun to gather early and already there were dozens of children underfoot, squealing and yelling and running clumsily in their costumes, a flock of little vampires and werewolves and skeletons and ghosts. The Ladies' Auxiliary of the V.F.W. had set up a table with hot coffee for the adults and hot chocolate for the children and plenty of orange-coated cookies, in the shapes of witches and pumpkins, for everyone. Later, there would be hot cider and other warming beverages for the adults.

Dale found his friend Jimmy almost at once.

"What happened to you today?" Jimmy asked. "You disappeared into thin air right after that club meeting."

"Yeah, I did, didn't I?" Dale said. He took a sip of his hot chocolate.

"So? What gives?"

"Wow, this hot chocolate is really great. Just hits the spot."

"Come on. What gives?"

"Boy, Jimmy, you know," Dale said thoughtfully, "this bonfire tonight's gonna be just as pretty as . . . Ireland's prettiest colleen."

"You're kidding," Jimmy said.

"I am not kidding."

"I need a drink," Jimmy said. He walked over to the Ladies' Auxiliary table, got a cup of hot chocolate, and returned.

"Wow," he said. "How far did you get?"

"Far enough."

"Are you going to see her tonight?"

"Is the moon made out of green cheese?"

"Wow. I mean, hey, wow. I mean, like, hey, I am seriously impressed. Colleen. Wow." He sipped his hot chocolate. "Poor me! I'll just have to suffer with Karen McCutchen."

"Karen McCutchen? Surely you jest."

Karen McCutchen—sometimes pronounced "McCookies"—was widely reputed among the young men of Deacons Kill to have the biggest pair of gazangas in two counties.

"Believe it," said Jimmy. "She's meeting me here tonight. That bonfire's not going to be the only thing burning around here."

And the two of them laughed and laughed and celebrated with more hot chocolate, and then they laughed some more. They shared the afternoon's intimacies with each other, and Jimmy had to admit that Dale's taking Colleen to the haunted house had been an inspiration, a serious inspiration, clearly beating out taking Karen to Prisco's Pizza.

Then Jimmy suddenly stopped laughing and began to look very thoughtful.

Dale knew that look. "Uh oh," he said. "You're about to commit an idea. Be careful. Don't hurt yourself."

"Dale, my friend, my basic buddy," Jimmy said, "I have just committed the most fantastic idea in the whole history of fantastic ideas. This time I've even outdone myself. Come on." He started away.

"What do you mean, 'come on'? The girls'll be here. They'll be looking for us."

"Not for another hour. But that's exactly why we have to get going, so we can get back quick, before the girls get here. Come on. We have work to do, places to go, things to get. Dale, I'm telling you, seriously, you're going to thank me for this for the rest of your life."

"That thing is humongous," Dale said. There was genuine reverence in his voice.

It was the biggest candle either one of them had ever seen. It was bright orange, round, a foot thick and four feet high, with a wick like a length of clothesline curling out of the tapered top.

They were in the back storeroom of Morgan's Hardware Supply on School Street, where Jimmy worked three afternoons a week and on Saturdays. He had the keys to open the door and to turn off the alarm, because he always had to go in ahead of opening time on Saturday to sweep up and straighten the stock.

"Where'd it come from?" Dale said.

"Some candle company sent it to Morgan," Jimmy told him. "I guess because he sold a zillion candles or something. He was supposed to put it in the window, I guess."

"Humongous," Dale said. "Also obscene."

"I knew you'd like it," Jimmy said. "Come on. We gotta hurry." He knelt beside the candle. "Come on."

"Exactly what is it you want to do with this thing, Einstein?"

Jimmy sighed dramatically. "I have to teach you everything, don't I? Okay, listen," he said, and he began to explain, but he'd barely started before Dale saw the light.

The two of them were laughing so hard that they nearly dropped the heavy candle as they struggled with it out the door.

A little over an hour later, accompanied by Colleen and Karen, they were starting up the pitch-black driveway to the haunted house.

"This is looking awfully familiar," Dale said.

"In more ways than one," Jimmy said.

The two of them chuckled.

"I think I'm a little scared," said Colleen. "This is creepy."

"What are you guys planning?" Karen said.

"Oh, nothing," Jimmy answered. "Nothing at all. You're in good hands, believe me. Heh, heh."

They all laughed, though the laughter was a little nervous.

"We should have brought flashlights," Colleen said.

The boys had been so preoccupied with the candle at Morgan's that they'd never thought of flashlights. Dale thought it was particularly generous of Colleen to phrase the comment the way she did.

They were having a hard time picking their way over the rough ground in the dark, but in a little while they emerged from the avenue of arching trees, and there was the house before them, washed in thin moonlight, a dark and blurry shadow against the nighttime sky.

"Creeparama!" breathed Karen.

Dale was thinking back suddenly to how the house had looked positively warm and inviting this afternoon, compared to the threatening way it seemed to loom above them now.

"It'll be great," Jimmy said, with hearty conviction. "Seriously. Besides, we've arranged a little surprise for you ladies."

"What's the surprise?" Karen immediately wanted to know.

"You'll see, you'll see," Jimmy told her. "All in good time. Just leave everything to me and my faithful Indian companion, Dale."

As they slogged across the final open distance toward the sagging front of the house, the girls paired off together, arms linked, with the two boys just behind them. Jimmy dug his elbow into Dale's side. But when they stood together at the bottom of the steps, Colleen once again took Dale's arm and he was emboldened to lead the way.

Busily supervising every step of the other three, paying particular attention to Colleen's safety, he led them up the swaying steps and across the rotting porch—it seemed noticeably less sturdy than before, or perhaps it was just showing the strain of additional weight—and into the open doorway of the house.

"Oh, yuck!" Karen said at once.

"It does smell worse than before, Dale," Colleen said quietly.

This was true. In fact, Dale had noticed the riper, richer smell of the house only an hour before when he'd been here, for the second time that day, with Jimmy. But then he'd been so out of breath from lugging the giant candle such a distance, and then wrestling it into the house and setting it up in the living room, that he really wasn't inclined to think too much about it. Now, on his third visit, he was unpleasantly aware that the air inside the house was indeed thick with an unpleasant, and still vaguely familiar, aroma.

"Well, we don't have to stay very long," he said.

Jimmy kicked his ankle.

They clung close together in the entryway, hesitating. It was impossible to see a thing. All around them, the darkness had a rich and fruity smell, not yet overpowering, but threatening to become so, given time.

"The door's been open since this afternoon," Dale said. "I guess the dampness just went to work on the house." This was definitely not the way he and Jimmy had envisioned things.

Colleen huddled against him and shivered.

"Maybe we should close the door," he said. "It'll keep out some of the cold. And the damp."

The others instantly agreed. Dale found the door and swung it shut. It closed with the same soft *plop* it had made when first opened that afternoon.

"Why don't you ladies go upstairs and explore?" Jimmy said. "There's a staircase just ahead on the right."

"How are we supposed to explore in the dark?" Karen asked. "I can't see a thing."

"I don't think we should," Colleen said.

Dale just wanted to get on with it. "It'll be okay," he told them. "Go ahead. Just go up for a minute. Jimmy and I have to get something ready down here."

Reluctantly, the girls groped their way forward until they found the banister.

"Oh, gross," Karen said out of the dark. "This railing is all sticky and wet."

"So is the wall," Colleen said. "It's all wet. And sort of soft."

"It's only the dampness," Jimmy said. "Go ahead. We'll call you in a second."

"I don't think I like this," they heard Karen saying from a few steps up. "Ick, the stairs feel like they're all mushy or something."

"Come on!" Jimmy snapped in Dale's ear, and they felt their

way into the living room. The walls down here felt wet and sticky too.

Bent forward, with their hands sweeping the air before them, they quickly located the upright candle. They knelt beside it at the same instant and, at the same instant, the two of them cried out. The floor where they had knelt was awash in some thick and chilly wetness that immediately soaked their jeans. At the same time, a new wave of the strange odor, even riper than it was in the hall, rose up to meet them.

"This is grossing me out," Dale said. "Seriously, Jimmy."

"I've got the matches," Jimmy said quickly. "At least we can see if there's a dry place."

The kitchen match flared, throwing flickering orange light and giant shifting shadows of themselves around the room. Jimmy touched it to the wick of the giant candle and, mercifully, the wick caught at once, burning with a bright and steady flame.

But their relief drained instantly away when they looked around the room. The walls themselves seemed to be rotting and sliding down toward the floor. Great stringy, ropy-looking things hung in dripping loops from the ceiling. The floor was covered with a pool of slick wetness, and everything glistened with some foul and smelly moisture.

They both held their breath for an instant, then Jimmy said, in a tone of genuine awe, "This is seriously disgusting."

Trying not to breathe too deeply, Dale said, "You can say that again."

"This is—"

But at that very moment, the two girls shrieked hysterically and came thudding down the stairs. One or both of them must have tripped—or more likely, slipped—and they both came crashing down in a tangle, landing with a splashing slide in the foyer.

The boys, breathing hard, slipped and slid over to them and helped them to their feet.

Sobbing, Colleen managed to say, "It's . . . It's as if the whole house was rotting away. My . . . my hand went right through the wall."

"It was all squishy," Karen managed to gasp. "Like the stairs. That's why we fell."

"What's that light?" Colleen asked suddenly. She lifted her head and looked all around. "Oh!" she gasped when she saw the slimy walls and the ropy things dripping from the ceiling.

"A candle," Jimmy said. "We got a candle."

"Let's get out of here," Dale said.

Without another word, the four of them rushed to the door. Dale pulled at the doorknob but the door would not budge. He tried again, then Jimmy pushed him aside and tried too, but with no success. When they looked more carefully at the door, they saw that it had sort of melted and run, becoming one with the wall all around it.

The girls were sobbing now and the boys were doing their best not to. Everywhere they looked, the house seemed to shift slightly. The angles in corners and the line where wall met ceiling were no longer sharp or clear. Everything was subtly moving, and more and more of the ropy things were dropping from the ceiling, making a tangled web all around them. They backed into the living room—at least there was some light in there—just as the staircase collapsed entirely with a wet, sucking sound. It brought down part of the upstairs floor with it, enough to seal off the entrance to the living room with a slimy, stinking heap. A glance showed that the windows here had blended into the walls, the same way the front door had. They were trapped.

Then they realized, in the light of the candle, what none of them had had time to notice before. The entire inside of the house had been painted—if it had actually once been paint—a startling and vivid shade of orange. But no, they realized at once with horror, it wasn't orange. It was even worse. It was pumpkin.

"Put out the candle," Colleen whispered. "Maybe that will help."

Jimmy pinched it out, but the darkness was even worse. It enhanced their other senses and they were horribly aware of the sound of softly sliding walls, liquid splashing as it dripped from above, and the thick smell in the air.

"Light it again," Dale whispered. "At least we'll have some light."

Jimmy relit the candle and they clung to one another. Now there was nothing left to do but wait. They huddled together, trembling, as the house, filled with the guttering light of the melting candle, and giving forth more and more of that same faintly sweet odor of decaying vegetable matter, slowly rotted and collapsed in around them.

Introduction:

Three Faces of the Night

BY CRAIG SHAW GARDNER

It's not easy to win a following by writing only short stories, but Craig Shaw Gardner is doing it. Among his varied tales are a fantasy series about Ebenezum, a wizard who's allergic to magic, "God's Eyes," a science fiction–horror story, and "Kisses from Aunty," a wonderfully unpleasant little shocker. He is also well known for his reviews of fantasy and science fiction in the Cleveland *Plain Dealer* and the Washington *Post,* and his film review column in *Fantasy Review.* His first novel, *A Malady of Magicks,* was recently published. Except when he's writing, he leads a reasonably normal life in Cambridge, Massachusetts.

"Three Faces of the Night" is one of his longest stories. It has enough darkness in it, most appropriate for Halloween, for half a dozen stories.

Three Faces of the Night

BY CRAIG SHAW GARDNER

I know you won't kill me yet.

You have to understand. It was green there. Greener than anything you can possibly imagine. No, don't laugh. I'll show you, if you insist.

Imagine a place unspoiled by neon signs or buildings or car exhaust or people, a place unsullied by any of those things we've grown to expect in a couple of thousand years of civilization. Think of a forest, then. Not a dark, forbidding wood, but a field filled with young saplings, each covered with buds and new, green leaves. Not a dark wood, no; a bright forest. And you walk into that forest on the edge of spring, on that day when winter has finally given way to the sun. And that new, warm air surrounds you, and pushes you with an energy you had thought lost with childhood.

Think of that, for a moment, while I talk.

It wasn't my fault. It was very important for me to realize that. I always blame myself for everything.

You know, my breakdown really helped me. Funny how I can say that now. Oh, I never want to be that upset again, that's for damn sure. But I realize now how much better I am for being crazy for a little while. I needed to go through that pain so that I could really see what was going on.

I knew you'd find me eventually. I'm surprised it took as long as it did. But those three years really gave me time to find myself, see that there was a world out there beyond Lenore. Other women find me attractive, you know? They think I'm funny. They're comfortable with me. They even tell me how mature I seem; very settled for my age. That's the biggest laugh of all. I never thought anyone would call me mature.

So Lenore sent you to watch over me? That's all? No rough stuff? So I'm still that important to you. What did she say about me? "Don't listen to a word Colin says. He'll just try to twist everything around. You know what he can do." Why else would you be waiting for her? You *are* waiting for Lenore?

Oh. Excuse me. I must get the phone. I assume this is Lenore at last, telling me what this is all about.

I wish you wouldn't point that gun at me.

You know, I'm not afraid of any of you anymore. You've lost your power over me.

It really isn't my fault.

1

Tonight would be the best night of all.

Colin lifted his face up, eyes shut tight, and smiled at the sun. It had rained most of the week, but now the sun shone so hard Colin felt it might bring summer back. But the trees were bare of all but a few golden leaves, and a fresh breeze sprang up at his back, proving the coolness of the air, sun or no sun. Colin pushed his hands into his jacket pockets, and started for home.

"Hey, Colin!"

He looked around to see who called. The half-smile on his face froze when he saw Tom Donnelly and Jimmy Kepler bearing down on him.

"Going out tonight, Cole?"

"Yeah," he said. He started walking again, his eyes on the leaves that covered the sidewalk. Tom knew he didn't like to be called Cole.

"We're going out too, aren't we, Jimmy?" Colin glanced at Tom despite himself. The taller boy had a quick, nervous smile, a flash of white in a face covered by red blotches.

"Maybe Colin wants to come too, huh?" Tom poked at Jimmy with an eager index finger. "Nah, I forgot. He's got to go trick-or-treating!"

Jimmy laughed then, a noise that started low, but cracked and shifted to a high giggle. Jimmy's voice was changing. He didn't talk much these days.

"Aw, come on and smash a couple pumpkins!" Tom poked at

Colin now. "We're gonna cut Mrs. Richards' clothesline. She'll have stuff up to dry, too! And we'll T.P. the hedges in front of that creep Crawford's place."

Colin kept on walking. He didn't want to hear about all this. Tom and Jimmy always seemed to get away with their pranks, but he knew if they wanted him to come along, it was only to get him in trouble. If Colin was there when a window smashed, they'd have someone to blame. Or maybe they'd just leave one of his gloves next to some of their dirty work.

"Come on, Cole." Tom grabbed Colin's shoulder. "What are you, some kind of faggot? We'll show you what's real fun."

Colin jerked away from Tom's hand. Tom laughed, and reached for him again.

"No!" Colin screamed with such force that it startled even him. He spun to see the two other boys staring at his face. Tom's smile had disappeared.

"You want to do something about it, Cole?" Tom took a step toward him. Colin took a step away. The pimples danced as Tom's smile reappeared.

"Get away from him!"

All three boys jerked their heads in the direction of the shout. Colin realized he had walked farther than he thought. They were standing next to Crawford's hedge.

Creep Crawford glared at them across the bushes. "If you two boys try anything, it'll be trouble!" Crawford's voice was high and shrill. His eyes were wide, and his skin looked very pale in the late afternoon light. Crawford was almost completely bald, and for a moment Colin thought his face was not the color of flesh at all, but rather the dead white of the bone underneath.

"Yeah?" Tom said after a moment's silence. His voice sounded higher, too, as if he wanted to match Crawford's tone. "What are you going to do about it?"

"I'll call the police." Crawford's mouth set into a grim line. It made his round, wrinkled face look determined, even strong. Colin's gaze was drawn back to the old man's eyes.

"Yeah. Right." Tom and Jimmy had both turned away from Crawford's stare, Tom watching the sidewalk, Jimmy looking wistfully across the street, as if anyplace in the neighborhood would be better than where he was right now. "Hey, we'll talk to you later, right, Cole?" Tom gave Colin a final, threatening glance, then both he and Jimmy were off down the street.

"Trouble," Crawford remarked. He half frowned. With the boys gone, his face had lost its sudden strength. He nodded to himself, his head bobbing up and down like an egg boiling in water. He added, as if to himself, "The world was made for trouble." His eyes snapped to Colin. "Those boys are no good."

"Yeah," Colin replied, not knowing what else to say. He half wanted to thank the older man, and half wanted to run away from him. Colin wished the whole thing had never happened.

Everybody got that feeling around Crawford. That's why they called him "the Creep." Colin remembered a night, two Halloweens back, the only time he'd ever knocked on Crawford's door.

The door had opened on that night, and Crawford had stood there, staring at him. The Creep was not a tall man, nor was he particularly sturdy-looking. He was wearing a brown, terry-cloth robe that made him look even more skinny than he did in his street clothes, and his mouth had been a little open, uncertain, as if he'd never seen an eleven-year-old boy dressed as a pirate before.

Colin had found himself standing on the doorstep alone. The two boys who were doing the neighborhood with him had disappeared. He didn't realize they had deserted him until after he'd rung the bell. His eye patch made it hard enough to see where he was going, much less who was with him.

Colin thrust his shopping bag forward. "Trick-or-treat."

"Trick-or-treat," Crawford had repeated, as if the words were new to him. "Oh. Trick-or-treat!" He laughed. "Of course. Trick-or-treat! Just a moment, just a moment." He darted away from the door, leaving Colin looking at the empty hallway. "I'm afraid I'm not very well prepared for this. Moving into a new house, and all. I'm sure I'll do better next year."

Crawford held an apple in his hand. "It's cold out there. I should have asked you to step in for a minute. I never do think."

Colin pushed the bag forward again, anxious to get the apple and be off. Where could his friends have gone? They still had half the neighborhood to cover.

Crawford's pale hand still gripped the apple. He hadn't gotten the hint. Instead, he smiled.

"You're the Thompson boy, aren't you? Colin? I had a talk with your father the day after I moved in. Says you always have your nose in a book. He says you like the way-out stuff."

He laughed. "I'm like that, too. Always have been. I've got quite a collection. I've got autographs from Poe and Verne. Books on all sorts of things. Ancient wisdom, magic, subjects I think you'd like. There's one book about the Celts . . ."

He paused and coughed, embarrassed by his enthusiasm. More quietly, he added, "You should stop by someday and see it."

Crawford had taken a step back as he spoke. Colin thought the old man would go on forever! He wanted to jump into the hallway, grab the apple, and run away.

He wouldn't, of course. It would be impolite. More than that, though, Colin had the strangest feeling that, if he ever stepped inside the old man's hallway, he would be trapped there, and he'd never be able to get out again.

"Why not come in now?" Crawford's smile broke into a big, toothy grin. "It'll only take a minute."

"Gee, Mr. Crawford," Colin blurted out, "I'd really like to, but I've got friends waiting for me, and it's almost time for me to go home, and besides, my mother gets mad at me if I stay out too late."

"Oh," Crawford said as the smile fell from his face. "I see. Well, don't worry. I see you'll do all right. I'm sure we can get together some other time."

He tossed the apple into the bag.

"Happy Halloween," he had added.

The Creep said those words again now, startling Colin from his daydream memory.

"Happy Halloween. Don't let those hoodlums bother you."

Crawford had reached his hands across the hedge while Colin was lost in thought. One rested on Colin's shoulder like a pale, withered moth.

"This is your favorite night, remember? This is the night you can do just what you want to do. You know"—a smile spread across his wrinkled face again—"you and I are so very much alike."

"I have to go. Goodbye." Colin took off across the street at a run. He felt something cold inside him that went from the spot on his shoulder where the Creep had touched him straight down to the pit of his stomach. It was Crawford's smile that had really gotten him, though; those large, white teeth in that pale face.

Colin started to get mad at himself. He was too old to be scared! Across the street and half a block away from Crawford, he slowed down to a walk. It was all the fault of those two hoods, Tom and Jimmy. If only he hadn't run into them. They had forced him to walk over to Crawford's, made him go face to face with the Creep. He kicked at the leaves on the sidewalk. He hated Tom and Jimmy for pushing him around. They were the real faggots!

But he hated Crawford, too. The more Colin thought about him, the way he talked, the way he had reached out with his pale fingers, the more that cold, hard lump within Colin twisted and grew. The hoods might have beaten him up if the Creep hadn't been there. But oh, how he wished the Creep hadn't been there!

Colin started to run again. If he could just run hard enough and fast enough, well—what? Colin couldn't finish the thought. He wished all of them would just go away!

"Colin, finish your dinner!"

Colin looked down at his dinner plate. He'd pushed down one side of his mashed potatoes with his fork, and the gravy was rapidly mixing with the peas. He wasn't really hungry. Tonight was Halloween.

"Colin, you're not going anywhere until you eat something!"

Colin looked at the clock. Bob would be over in fifteen minutes. He forced a forkful into his mouth. The mashed potatoes were cold.

He glanced at his mother. Her mouth was a thin, hard line, her gaze unrelenting. He managed another forkful.

His mother looked away.

"Oh! Isn't she cute! Martin, let's take a picture!"

Colin's little sister walked down the stairs in her ballerina costume.

Colin glanced anxiously at the clock. "Mom, I gotta go!"

His mother began a lecture on eating habits that somehow segued into his insistence on trick-or-treating with a friend rather than escorting his little sister. Colin excused himself and jumped from the table.

"I don't know, Colin." His mother's words trailed him up the stairs. "I just don't know."

But Colin knew. This was his night, the best night of all. He opened his bedroom door, and smiled when he saw his costume laid across the bed.

He had gotten it all ready that afternoon. It had let him forget about Tom and Jimmy and Crawford. He could lose himself in Halloween.

He changed into his costume as fast as he could, tossing his jeans and sweater across the room to get them out of the way. Black pants, white shirt, an old black cloak he'd bought at the Salvation Army. And of course the plastic fangs. He'd first seen them in the back of a comic book, right between ads for the joy buzzer and the X-ray glasses that let you see through walls, clothes, everything! He slid the plastic over his upper teeth.

"I never drink—vine," he managed. The plastic slid around, making it hard to talk. Still, it would do.

He flipped off the light switch and walked back to the mirror. Yep. This was the best part.

His new fangs glowed bright green in the dark.

"Colin!" It was his father's voice. "Bob's here!"

Colin leaped from the room and bounded down the stairs three at a time, his cloak flapping behind him.

"Good heavens!" his father cried in horror. "It's the count!"

"I never drink—vine!" Colin repeated for his newfound audience.

Bob stood in the front hallway, wearing a torn sportcoat and a Frankenstein mask.

"Come on, Colin. Let's get going." Bob's voice was muffled by the rubber.

They ran from the house, followed by his mother's warning of dire consequences if he was not home by nine.

But they were out now, out in the night. And there was something about this night. On Halloween, Colin was free. He felt he could go wherever he wanted and be whoever he wanted to be. There was no way he could have taken his sister. Tonight he and Bob were kings of the neighborhood, but they were lonely kings, with no ties and no one to hold them down.

Colin spread his cape and howled. Bob shook his head and grumbled something behind his mask.

Colin took to swinging his bag back and forth as they went from house to house. The leaves crackled with joy beneath his feet, gravel leaped in the air when he kicked it. This got better every year.

It was different after dark. The night was clear and bright, a brilliant half-moon hanging in the sky. A dog barked somewhere across the street.

"Ah," Colin remarked. "The children of the night. What music they make."

Bob pulled off his Frankenstein mask to glare at him. Colin smiled. It wasn't every night you got to be a vampire. At the moment, his fangs were in his shirt pocket. It made it easier to talk between houses.

"If you make one more joke about biting," Bob remarked, "I'm going home."

Colin slipped his teeth back in as they stepped onto the Pittmans' porch. Mrs. Pittman remarked that maybe they were getting a little big for this sort of thing, but she still dropped the candy in their bags. The boys thanked her and hurried on.

The next house was Crawford's. By silent agreement, the boys passed without opening the front gate, lugging their heavy bags to the next house on the street.

Colin heard a rustling in the bushes. He stopped and looked across the hedge. The twisting cold was back inside him.

He saw long, white streamers hanging from the trees. Toilet paper. Tom and Jimmy must be in the Creep's yard.

A hand grabbed Colin's shirt through the bushes. Colin made a strangled sound in his throat. He was too scared to yell.

"Colin, what—" Bob began.

The hand pulled Colin into the hedge. Tom's face smiled at him.

"So you decided to come and help after all, huh?" the taller youth whispered. "Maybe you're not a faggot after all."

There was a shrill scream behind him. Tom's mouth hung open, his next words lost. The scream had come from Crawford's house.

Tom turned and ran.

Colin pushed his way through the bush after him.

He wasn't afraid anymore. His fear had turned to anger again. He was mad at Tom and Jimmy for doing whatever they had done to the old man. And he was mad at the Creep for saving him earlier that day, and making him feel responsible.

But Colin felt obligated now. He had to find out what they'd done to Crawford.

A figure stood in the yard, silhouetted by the light from the open front door. Tom had stopped his headlong flight to stare. It was Jimmy. He held something in front of him, and he was crying.

Both Tom and Colin walked toward him, the night silent save for Jimmy's sobs. He held an open scout knife in his hands. The blade was black in the moonlight. There was black on Jimmy's shirt, too. Blood.

Jimmy stared at Tom.

"I fell on it," he said. The tears stopped at the sight of his friend. "He was calling me. He knew my name. I got scared, and tripped and fell down the stairs. I didn't know the knife was open. I cut myself."

The blood on his shirt shone wet in the moonlight. He was still bleeding. Jimmy began to cry more softly.

"We got to get out of here," Tom said. He turned to go. Jimmy made no move to follow. "Come on, faggot, move!"

Jimmy took a hesitant step forward.

"Colin." Crawford's voice called him quietly from inside the house.

Colin turned to look at the brightly lit doorway, the cheerful golden windows, all thoughts of Tom and Jimmy gone from his mind. Crawford had called him, even though Colin hadn't said a word since he'd come into the yard. How did the Creep know he was there?

He walked toward the house. Jimmy's sobs faded behind him. Crawford did not call him again. Maybe, Colin thought, he had never called him at all.

He still carried his trick-or-treat bag, heavy with the prizes from the neighborhood. Colin left it sitting on the welcome mat as he walked into the front hallway.

There was a pool of blood on the tile. Dark brown spots zigzagged up the carpeted stairway in front of him.

Colin went up the stairs.

There was only one light shining on the second floor. The door was open. Colin saw white tile. The bathroom. His feet made no sound on the thick carpet as he approached, the floor beneath him part of his walking dream.

He stopped when he saw Crawford.

The Creep lay naked in a bathtub filled with blood. No. It wasn't dark enough for blood. Dark red water, then. Crawford had been bleeding into the bathwater for some time. His eyes were closed. He lay very still. His skin had been dyed pink from the bloody water. It gave his face and shoulders a ruddy look, so much more healthy-looking than his pale white flesh.

Colin took a step into the room.

Crawford opened his eyes.

Colin felt everything stop. He couldn't speak, he couldn't breathe, he couldn't move.

Crawford rose from the bathtub. Blood pumped from slits at both his wrists.

"I'm glad you came to visit, Colin." He smiled. His teeth were still pale white. "I knew you would. You and I, Colin, we're very much alike."

Crawford stepped from the tub.

"We share things that other people will never know." His voice was soft but clear, as if he were discussing the weather. "We have power that other people do not. We can use knowledge. What use have scum like those boys for knowledge?"

Crawford walked toward Colin. The Creep's legs trembled violently. "I'm glad we have this chance to talk. There are things I've wanted to pass on to you. Things scum would never understand." His foot slipped a bit on the bathroom tile. Somehow, he managed to keep his balance.

"Forever and ever. I thought it would never end. Hundreds and hundreds and hundreds. But it gets harder all the time. So hard. Have I waited too long?" He sighed. "Perhaps it's always too late. You'll understand that, when you're older."

Crawford took a deep breath.

"I have a gift for you, Colin." His smile was gentle as he lifted his bleeding wrists to Colin's mouth.

"Taste my life, Colin. Then you'll know."

Crawford dragged his wrists toward the boy's mouth. Colin felt dampness on his cheek. He jerked his head back, the plastic fangs falling from his mouth.

Crawford nodded at the blood pouring from both his wrists.

"This way," he said, "it takes a very, very long time to die."

Colin felt warm, as if he had a fever. He backed away from Crawford, but every step he took increased the heat. The Creep fell to his knees. The old man's eyes were full of fear.

"Not like this," he whispered. "I didn't know it would be like this . . ."

The heat washed over Colin. He shivered with its intensity. There was a roaring in his ears. He shut his eyes and swayed.

Colin stood in a field at night. The stars above him were the brightest he had ever seen. He felt his heartbeat, slow in his chest, and listened to his breathing as his lungs took in air sweeter than anything he had ever tasted.

It was quiet here, but not silent. Night birds called and insects rubbed their wings. Small animals ran through the grass at his feet, while others clung to the branches of the young trees that surrounded him, trees that would one day make this place a forest.

Why was he here? Colin didn't know, but somehow it didn't matter. He felt like he belonged here, like this place was made for him and him alone.

The birds and insects and animals called out and welcomed him. The trees swayed in greeting, the stars sang overhead, the grass whispered his name.

Somewhere, far off, he heard a creature whimper.

Suddenly cold, he opened his eyes. Crawford lay before him on the tile, face down. His wrists no longer bled.

Colin ran.

So where was I?

Oh. I see your smile. You never were very good at hiding things. I could always tell what you were thinking, even back when we were kids. You think you know everything, but there's so much you and the others never bothered with. Mr. Know-it-all. That's why Lenore sent you here, you and your gun. It must be sad to need a gun so badly.

What have I got to complain about? Oh, don't get defensive on me, it would be out of character. "But we always treated you well." That's your next line, right? Well, you did treat me in a way that suited your purpose. It even kept me happy for a little while. More important, it kept me from asking questions.

I have to be responsible to myself. I guess that's the biggest lesson that this pain has taught me. I had to get over my own fear. Big deal, huh? Well, let me talk. It passes the time until Lenore gets here, right?

If you had told me the truth from the first, it might have been different. Oh, I know you didn't want another Crawford. Too independent. But Crawford was right. Scum like you could never understand what he and I knew.

Point that gun the other way, won't you, Tom? And think about that forest again. We'll need it for tonight.

Yeah, I can still do it. Don't worry your old, bald head. I just have to cut a little deeper, is all. But I have a lot of miles left, believe me. I've been practicing. I'm much better than I was before.

I've seen Lenore, you know. From a distance. I had to. When you're so close to someone for so long—

It was a shock to me to see how gray she's gotten. She must be desperate to see me.

Will you let me live after you've used me?

Oh, should I get the door? Okay, go ahead, you do it. I imagine this will be Lenore. How many more did she bring?

I should live, you know. It really isn't my fault.

2

The city was different after dark.

Colin had walked to Lenore's new apartment a couple of times during the daylight. It was a busy street, then, with people everywhere, walking in and out of the neighborhood shops, sitting in the park across the way to talk or eat their lunch.

Now all the stores were closed. The park was a dark, empty place, watched over by a dozen bare trees whipped about by the night wind. There wasn't any traffic. The street was a vast expanse of barren asphalt, empty, incapable of life, as if someone had paved the surface of the moon.

Colin felt very alone. That was the last thing he wanted tonight. He hurried down the alleyway to Lenore's place.

"Trick-or-treat," he said as the door opened.

"Hey, man." A.J., a kid from his dorm, stood in the doorway. He pushed his wire-rims back up his skinny nose. "Only tricks here, you know? Come on in and join the party."

Colin threw his coat on a pile by the door. When he looked back up, A.J. had disappeared into the crowd.

The press of people around him threatened to panic him as surely as his loneliness outside. He shouldn't let Julie upset him like that. After all, that's why he'd come to Lenore's party. He'd have a good time. That was what Halloween was all about, right?

"Colin!" Lenore wove between the bodies that already crowded the kitchen. She'd decorated this room in bright reds and yellows. Windowsills and cupboard doors were painted in alternating colors, pulling Colin's gaze away from the Indian print dresses and flowered shirts that cluttered the room. Lenore's parties were always a feast for eye and ear. Colin had to grin. This roomful of bodies looked half like a circus and half like some medieval painter's view of hell.

"I'm so glad you came!" Lenore smiled as she approached. She had freed her red hair from its usual braid. It fell in waves across her shoulders and caressed her arms, the ends just touching the curve of her hips. She was dressed in her usual black, but tonight her skirt was made of leather.

She rested a hand on Colin's shoulder.

"Did you come alone?"

"Alone?" Colin asked, aware of the way her fingers played against his collarbone. "Oh, sure. That's all over now."

"Well, of course, it's none of my business." Lenore allowed herself a Mona Lisa smile. "But I'm glad."

"Hey! Come on, Lenore." A.J. waved an unlit joint in their direction. Lenore grabbed Colin's hand and pulled him after her.

"Hey, man." A.J. nodded at him and smiled. His wire-rims slid down his nose every time he moved his head. "Welcome to the real party!"

Colin looked around the room as he was led through the door. A dozen or so people sat or sprawled on the floor. It was hard to see their faces. The walls of the room had been painted black, and the only light came from a cluster of candles at the room's center.

This looked like a group all set to get stoned. Well, Colin thought, why not? It would save him the trouble of answering questions about Julie.

What was the matter with that girl, anyway? He couldn't stop thinking about her. He could still see her face, so angry he could hardly recognize her.

"No!" she had screamed. "You will not!"

"Don't tell me what I can do! I'll do whatever I want!" He was shouting, too. There was something about her these days that enraged him. Somehow, it was all different now.

When he and Julie had first started to go steady, back in high school, Colin thought that he had really fallen in love. He had thought the two of them would go on forever. He'd gone away to college, and the first half of his freshman year had been the loneliest time of his life. When Julie decided to transfer to Boston for her sophomore year, he couldn't have been happier.

Now he didn't know what love was. What the two of them had together back home wasn't the same here in Boston. Julie didn't like Colin's new friends. What had happened to the quiet, studious boy she knew in high school? He had to be nicer to her parents on the phone. And his hair was too long. After all, weren't the two of them going to get married?

And all they did now was fight.

Somebody passed Colin a joint. It was rolled with red, white, and blue paper, like the American flag.

Colin inhaled the smoke in little gasps, careful to keep from coughing. He'd only smoked a couple of times before. He wasn't really sure if he'd ever been truly stoned. This time, maybe, he'd let it all out, go all the way. He felt like he really needed it.

"Hey, Colin." Lenore was at his side again, smiling up into his face. He liked Lenore's dimples. "Why don't you sit down and relax? You take things too seriously."

Lenore sat beside him. "I like you, Colin." She reached out to touch his hand. "I can talk to you."

He smiled at that. Julie would never say something like that to him.

"We're all friends here." She made a sweeping gesture to include the whole circle. "I'll introduce you." She began to recite names. Colin nodded, not really listening.

"This is a very special night, you know." She paused to take a drag from the joint, then passed it on to Colin. "I wanted my party on Halloween for a special reason."

Lenore shifted her place on the floor so that one of her black-stockinged legs leaned against Colin's knee.

"Do you know about Halloween, Colin?" She drew a pointed pattern on the floor with one scarlet fingernail. "I mean the real Halloween. Not just trick-or-treating, but where it all comes from. All Hallows' Eve—"

"Hey, Lenore." A.J. squatted down next to the two of them.

"We've gone through the first three joints. Want me to bring out the hash?"

"Sounds good to me." She squeezed Colin's knee as A.J. left. "He tells me this is really good stuff."

Colin nodded absently as he studied the other faces in the room. A lot of people from the dorm usually came to Lenore's parties. Colin didn't always know everybody's name, but half the people generally looked familiar. This room was filled with strangers.

"I've found out some fascinating things about Halloween," Lenore continued. "True things. Things people knew a long time ago. There's so much that's been lost, Colin. But, if we really work at it, we can get it back."

Lenore puffed on a joint that appeared from nowhere. She passed it on to Colin. Her words rang in his ears as he inhaled. "We've gotten too far from nature, Colin. Too far from the Earth. Nature holds power, power that we lose when we live in cities like this. But we can call that power to us if we try hard enough."

She squeezed his shoulder gently. "Help us, Colin. Everyone, think of a forest. A young, healthy forest, growing, full of the power of the Earth."

Colin let his mind fill with the image of young woods. He was surprised how easy it was to call forth that picture. When was the last time he had been in a forest?

"Let's have some music!" Lenore called. Someone put on a record in the other room. Jefferson Airplane. *After Bathing at Baxter's.* "A Small Package of Value Will Come to You Shortly." Colin nodded his head to the music and the voices. It made him smile.

Lenore gripped his arm. She was smiling, too. "Ah, you're beginning to feel it. Try this."

She put a silver pipe to his mouth. Blue flame danced from a match she held over the bowl as Colin inhaled. Warm smoke filled his lungs with a pleasant pressure. He held it inside as long as he could.

"Oh, hey, there's somebody here from your old hometown. I meant to tell you." She ran her hand lightly down Colin's sleeve. It made his arm tingle. "I'm afraid I'm not a very good hostess."

She sprawled across the center of the room, careful not to disturb the circle of candles, and hit another guy's knee. The owner of the knee leaned forward into the light.

"Hey, Tom. You're from Irondequoit, right?"

Tom Donnelly.

It took Tom a minute to answer the question. He didn't look at them. His eyes didn't seem to focus anywhere in particular.

He nodded at last. "Yeah," he said softly.

Lenore repositioned herself next to Colin. She wore an expression of total delight, as if this were the greatest surprise anyone had ever had.

"You know Tom, right?"

"Sure," Colin said. "Hi, Tom." He hadn't seen Tom in years. The Donnellys had moved away soon after that night at Crawford's.

"Yeah?" Tom blinked. His eyes turned to regard Colin. "Hey, Cole," he said, and for an instant his face was lit by the smile Colin had learned to hate. Then Tom coughed, his face slack again. Someone passed him the pipe. Tom sucked hungrily at it, as if he were a drowning man and the smoke were oxygen.

"See?" Lenore said. "You never know who you're going to meet at my parties."

For some reason, Colin thought of Julie again. Mention of his hometown, he guessed. He always seemed to be thinking of Julie.

"Don't you dare go to that party!" She had seen Lenore. She flew into a rage when Colin mentioned the other girl's name. The two women had had a "conversation." Julie wouldn't tell Colin what was said.

Her anger fired his in turn. That's the way it always worked. There was no room for talking anymore, only shouting.

"I'll do what I want!"

"Colin, why are you doing this to me? I don't know what you want anymore!"

"Well, I guess you never knew me at all, did you?"

"Colin, if you go to that party, I'm going to come after you and drag you out!"

"You do, and I'll never talk to you again!"

She had started to cry somewhere around then, and her tears had washed Colin's anger away. He did love her, that was the funny thing. He couldn't think of going through life without her. Why couldn't they talk anymore?

"Why what, Colin?"

Colin blinked. A woman's face floated above him.

"Julie?"

"No, silly. You're really stoned, aren't you?" Lenore kissed him lightly on the forehead. He reached for her hand. The contact, flesh on flesh, calmed him.

"Let's talk for a while," Lenore said, moving close by his side.

Colin let her do the talking. He liked to hear the sound of her voice. She told him about old wisdom: the sound of a rushing stream, the force of a tree reaching to the sky, the solid pressure of earth underneath your feet. The ancients had known about these things, had known them to be as alive as any man or animal, with a spirit and power all their own. And this was the night, the end of the Celtic year, the time to honor them. And they would honor you in turn.

Colin loved sharing Lenore's excitement as she talked about new things. She wasn't stuck in one place like Julie. Lenore went out to get her own apartment. Sure, it wasn't in the best neighborhood, but Lenore had really fixed it up.

Colin found his attention wandering. Lenore was saying something about the way the candles were placed in the room, and what it all meant. He wanted to listen to her, he really did, but there were so many other things to look at, to hear, to smell. The stereo played a song about Saturday afternoon. Colin could feel the bassline ripple through his muscles.

Lenore was running her hand lightly up and down his thigh. This set up another rhythm inside him, pulsating against the music. Lenore was talking about this, the most important of nights. Colin closed his eyes, but the rhythms were too strong. They threatened to overwhelm him, carry him away. Suddenly afraid, he opened his eyes.

The people looked different now. They had no depth, they were flat, like pictures pasted on the walls of the room. When they moved, they walked and talked in slow motion, as if they were movies projected onto Colin's eyes.

But the strange sights somehow calmed him. He was hallucinating, that was all. There must have been something stronger than usual in whatever he'd smoked. That had to be it. Lenore was with him. He'd be all right. He just needed to sit back and enjoy the ride.

He felt dampness on the end of his finger. The pain came later, distanced, removed.

There was a round, dark spot on his index finger. Lenore had scratched him with a penknife.

"It's time for the offering." She smiled as she spoke. He liked her smile. It took the pain away.

"Offering?"

"Yes, we can go there now. To the forest, the source of life. They want us there now on the last day of harvest."

"You're like some kind of magician." Colin shook his head. The world spun around him.

A.J.'s smiling face swept into view. "She calls herself a priestess."

"A priestess?" Colin thought of the blood on his finger. "Am I the offering?"

"No, no, silly." Lenore's voice was soothing. "I'd never offer you to anybody. If I'm a priestess, then you're my King of the Wood."

Her hands covered Colin's. She kissed him. "Now think of a forest, my king . . ."

Colin's lips tingled where Lenore had kissed him. He needed to kiss her again. The other people in the room were saying something, over and over again. He couldn't understand the words. Just how stoned was he?

Then he was standing in the forest. His forest: the one he had dreamed about. The forest he had walked through before.

When he first came here, he had thought of it as a field dotted with trees. Now the oaks around him had matured. Although far from fully grown, they were a presence around him. He could feel their strength as he strode between them. His feet knew the peace of the grass, and the serenity of the earth beneath.

A small bird cried from a tree. Its wing had caught in a branch. The feathers hung limp at the dark bird's side. Colin found himself fascinated with the small creature's struggle. The bird staggered, trying vainly to fly with one good wing. It fell to earth.

There was a crash on the street below, and a scream.

"What?" Colin blinked in the candlelight. The sound of breaking glass echoed in his ears.

"It's nothing, Colin dearest." Lenore began to unbutton his shirt. "Just someone having fun on Halloween. You're very special, Colin," she whispered as she laid a trail of kisses across his neck and cheek. "There have been others, but they've always disappointed us. The last one chose you." She kissed his forehead, his eyebrows, his eyelids. "You will be so fine."

Colin heard another scream.

"No!" he yelled, lurching away from Lenore's embrace. He stood, but had trouble keeping his balance. He thought of other screams on another night, when he was a boy. He didn't want that to happen again.

There were other sharp sounds outside the window. He was sure he could hear them behind the voices. He had to go out there.

"Colin, no!" Lenore materialized at his side. He was aware of her breast against his arm. "It has to be . . ." She paused. "I need you with me tonight."

Colin felt himself begin to respond to her touch. But the noise was still there in his head. He couldn't tell what was real.

He cleared his throat. "I'll be back in a minute." He had to see if anything was there. Lenore grabbed for his arm, but he slipped between her fingers.

The world was a jumble of indistinct shapes. A dozen shades of blue blurred together. Objects tilted crazily as he tried to steady himself.

He wasn't afraid. Somehow, in the back of his mind, that surprised him. He was angry instead; angry with Julie, angry at Tom, angry about that night at Crawford's, angry at the world. His anger gave him purpose, made him put one foot in front of the other. He closed his eyes and kept on walking.

Somehow, he made it down the stairs and opened the front door. The cold air hit him like rainwater. He suddenly saw the street with crystal clarity, the streetlights as bright as the sun.

Someone lay huddled and bleeding on the pavement. He recognized the coat she wore.

"Julie?" Colin whispered.

A figure fled from the shadows and ran past Colin, moving in that nervous, frightened way that Tom had run that night at Crawford's. The fugitive's face was distorted by the fear Colin could not feel.

"Colin?"

Dully, Colin turned around.

Lenore was there. She wrapped her arms around him, pressed herself close. Her leg rubbed against his. She kissed him. Her lips were moist and dark and tasted of salt. Her kiss burned. Shivers of warmth billowed through his body.

She held a glass, filled with dark liquid. Colin drank.

"Come with me," she whispered.

The forest was in him again. He was the forest, the sturdy trees, the grass, the air, the birds and insects and animals. He was filled with the warmth of the sun.

"You're with us now, Colin," Lenore said from a great distance away.

Colin followed the sound of her voice.

You don't have to hit me. I know what you're here for. It's Halloween again, and you need me.

It's a shame, Lenore. We didn't always talk like this. Remember when we were first married? That was a long time ago, though.

Tell Tom to point his gun away. Time for your King of the Wood to do his job. Does anyone have a knife?

I've been studying this for a while. I don't think this will reverse anything, just slow things down again. I'm afraid, Lenore, you can never be as young as I am again.

Ow. There, it's done. I have to cut deeper every time. I need more blood to make it work. I guess I'm getting closer to Crawford all the time.

You can stop threatening me now. Are you going to kill me when this is all over? I assume you've found a replacement, Lenore. After all, I won't follow orders. But you've lost sight of so many things. It really isn't my fault.

Okay, okay. I'll shut up.

Everyone should think of the forest.

Colin walked into the cool wood. His wood. He knew every tree now, its shape and height and strength. There were sturdy oaks all around him, and each of them had power. Pure air filled his lungs. This was his forest, and the forest was eternal. He gave to the wood, and the wood gave back to him. Lenore was right. King of the Wood.

He caused the roots to move in that way he had learned, and made them catch small animals that scurried along the ground. A branch whipped high in a tree, striking a bird that fell with a single cry. It was caught in the roots as well. Roots encircled all the creatures now, and tightened around them.

Colin could feel the warmth again. It filled him, the sun on his back, in his face, in his blood.

He was King of the Wood. He'd be forever young. He was so full of the forest, he could barely hear their screams.

When he opened his eyes at last, he was alone. The others were so torn apart now that you would never know there had once been whole bodies in this room. It had, of course, ruined the carpet, but that was easily replaced.

He wasn't afraid anymore. He hadn't been for a while, now. Poor people. They had wanted to control the King of the Wood, and stay forever young. Well, they wouldn't age anymore.

He looked sadly down at a bit of what might have been Lenore. "It really isn't my fault," he said. "This way, it takes a very, very long time to die."

Introduction:

Pumpkin

BY BILL PRONZINI

Mystery writer Bill Pronzini concocts his dark puzzles in the bright sunshine of California's Bay Area. He is best known for his psychological thrillers, like *Masques,* and for his popular mystery novels featuring the Nameless Detective, who, though nameless, resembles Pronzini more than a little. He has also edited a lively series of horror anthologies with titles like *Creature!, Mummy!, Voodoo!,* and *Werewolf!*

And now, at Halloween, it's time to beware . . . Pumpkin!

Pumpkin

BY BILL PRONZINI

The pumpkin, the strange pumpkin, came into Amanda Sutter's life on a day in late September.

She had spent most of that morning and early afternoon shopping in Half Moon Bay, and it was almost two o'clock when she pointed the old Dodge pickup south on Highway One. She watched for the sign, as she always did; finally saw it begin to grow in the distance, until she could read, first, the bright orange letters that said SUTTER PUMPKIN FARM, and then the smaller black letters underneath: *The Biggest, The Tastiest, The Best—First Prize Winner, Half Moon Bay Pumpkin Festival, 1976.*

Amanda smiled as she turned past the sign, onto the farm's unpaved access road. The wording had been Harley's idea, which had surprised some people who didn't know him very well. Harley was a quiet, reserved man—too reserved, sometimes; she was forever trying to get him to let his hair down a little—and he never bragged. As far as he was concerned, though, the sign was simply a statement of fact. "Well, our pumpkins *are* the biggest, the tastiest, the best," he'd said when one of their neighbors asked him about it. "And we *did* win first prize in '76. If the sign said anything else, it'd be a lie."

That was Harley for you. In a nutshell.

The road climbed up a bare-backed hill, and when she reached the crest Amanda stopped the pickup to admire the view. She never tired of it, especially at this time of year and on this sort of crisp, clear day. The white farm buildings lay in a little pocket directly below, with the fields stretching out on three sides and the ocean vast and empty beyond. The pumpkins were ripe now, the same bright orange as the lettering on the sign—Connecticut Field for the most part, with a single parcel devoted to Small

Sugar; hundreds of them dotting the brown and green earth like a bonanza of huge gold nuggets, gleaming in the afternoon sun. The sun-glare was caught on the ruffly blue surface of the Pacific, too, so that it likewise carried a sheen of orange-gold.

She sat for a time, watching the Mexican laborers Harley had hired to harvest the pumpkins—to first cut their stems and then, once they had had their two-to-three weeks of curing in the fields, load the bulk of the crop onto produce trucks for shipment to San Francisco and San Jose. It wouldn't be long now before Halloween. And on the weekend preceding it, the annual Pumpkin Festival.

The festival attracted thousands of people from all over the Bay Area and was the year's big doings in Half Moon Bay. There was a parade featuring the high school band and kids dressed up in Halloween costumes; there were booths selling crafts, whole pumpkins, and pumpkin delicacies—pies and cookies, soups and breads; and on Sunday the competition between growers in the area for the season's largest exhibition pumpkin was held. The year Sutter Farm had won the contest, 1976, the fruit Harley had carefully nurtured in a mixture of pure compost and spent-mushroom manure weighed in at 236 pounds. There had been no blue ribbons since, but the prospects seemed good for this season: one of Harley's new exhibition pumpkins had already grown to better than 240 pounds.

Amanda put the Dodge in gear and drove down the road to the farmyard. When she came in alongside the barn she saw Harley talking to one of the laborers, a middle-aged Mexican whose name, she remembered, was Manuel. No, not talking, she realized as she shut off the engine—arguing. She could hear Manuel's raised voice, see the tight, pinched look Harley always wore when he was annoyed or upset.

She went to where they stood. Manuel was saying, "I will not do it, Mr. Sutter. I am sorry, I will not."

"Won't do what?" Amanda asked.

Harley said, "Won't pick one of the pumpkins." His voice was pitched low but the strain of exasperation ran through it. "He says it's haunted."

"What!"

"Not haunted, Mr. Sutter," Manuel said. "No, not that." He turned appealing eyes to Amanda. "This pumpkin must not be picked, *señora.* No one must cut its stem or its flesh, no one must eat it."

"I don't understand, Manuel. Whyever not?"

"There is something . . . I cannot explain it. You must see this pumpkin for yourself. You must . . . feel it."

"Touch it, you mean?"

"No, Mrs. Sutter. *Feel* it."

Harley said, "You've been out in the sun too long, Manuel."

"This is not a joke, *señor,*" Manuel said in grave tones. "The other men do not feel it as strongly as I, but they also will not pick this pumpkin. We will all leave if it is cut, and we will not come back."

Amanda felt a vague chill, as if someone had blown a cold breath against the back of her neck. She said, "Where is this pumpkin, Manuel?"

"The east field. Near the line fence."

"Have you seen it, Harley?" she asked her husband.

"Not yet. We might as well go out there, I guess."

"Yes," Manuel said. "Come with me, see for yourself. *Feel* for yourself."

Amanda and Harley got into the pickup; Manuel had driven in from the fields in one of the laborers' flatbed trucks, and he led the way in that. They clattered across the hilly terrain to the field farthest from the farm buildings, to its farthest section near the pole-and-barbed-wire line fence. From there, Manuel guided them on foot among the rows of big trailing vines with their heart-shaped leaves and their heavy ripe fruit. Eventually he stopped and pointed without speaking. Across a barren patch of soil, a single pumpkin grew by itself, on its own vine, no others within five yards of it.

At first Amanda noticed nothing out of the ordinary; it seemed to be just another Connecticut Field, larger than most, a little darker orange than most. But then she moved closer, and she saw that it was . . . different. She couldn't have said quite how it was different, but there was something . . .

"Well?" Harley said to Manuel. "What about it?"

"You don't feel it, *señor?*"

"No. Feel what?"

But Amanda felt it. She couldn't have explained that either; it was just . . . an aura, a sense of something emanating from the pumpkin that made her uneasy, brought primitive little stirrings of fear and disgust into her mind.

"I do, Harley," she said, and hugged herself. "I know what he means."

"You too? Well, I still say it's nonsense. I'm going to cut it and be done with it. Manuel, let me have your knife . . ."

Manuel backed away, putting his hand over the sharp harvesting knife at his belt. "No, Mr. Sutter. No. You must not!"

"Harley," Amanda said sharply, "he's right. Leave it be."

"Damn. Why should I?"

"It is evil," Manuel said, and looked away from the pumpkin and made the sign of the cross. "It is an evil thing."

"Oh for God's sake. How can a pumpkin be evil?"

Amanda remembered something her uncle, who had been a Presbyterian minister, had said to her when she was a child: *Evil takes many forms, Mandy. Evil shares our bed and eats at our own table. Evil is everywhere, great and small.*

She said, feeling chilled, "Harley, I don't know how, I don't know why, but that pumpkin *is* an evil thing. Leave it alone. Let it rot where it lies."

Manuel crossed himself again. "Yes, *señora!* We will cover it, hide it from the sun, and it will wither and die. It can do no harm if it lies here untouched."

Harley thought they were crazy; that was plain enough. But he let them have their way. He sat in the truck while Manuel went to get a piece of milky plastic rain sheeting and two other men to help him. Amanda stood near the front fender and watched the men cover the pumpkin, anchor the sheeting with wooden stakes and chunks of rock, until they were finished.

Harley had little to say during supper that night, and soon afterward he went out to his workshop in the barn. He was annoyed at what he called her "foolishness," and Amanda couldn't really blame him. The incident with the pumpkin had already taken on a kind of surreal quality in her memory, so that she had begun to think that maybe she and Manuel and the other workers *were* a pack of superstitious fools.

She went out to sit on the porch, bundled up in her heavy wool sweater, as night came down and blacked out the last of the sunset colors over the ocean. An evil pumpkin, she thought. Good Lord, it was ridiculous—a Halloween joke, a sly fantasy tale for children like those that her father used to tell of ghosts and goblins, witches and warlocks, things that go bump in the dark Halloween night. How could a pumpkin be evil? Pumpkins were an utterly harmless fruit: you made pies and cookies from them, you carved them into grinning jack-o'-lanterns; they were a symbol of a grand old tradition, a happy children's rite of fall.

And yet . . .

When she concentrated she could picture the way the strange pumpkin had looked, feel again the vague aura of evil that radiated from it. A small shiver passed through her. Why hadn't Harley felt it too? Some people just weren't sensitive to auras and emanations, she supposed that was it. He was too practical, too logical, too much of a skeptic—a true son of Missouri, the "Show Me" state. He simply couldn't understand.

Understand what? she thought then. I don't understand it either. I don't even know what it is that I'm afraid of.

How did the damned thing get there? Where did it come from? What *is* it?

She found herself looking out toward the east field, as if the pumpkin might somehow be pulsing and glowing under its plastic covering, lighting up the night. There was nothing to see but darkness, of course. Silly. Ridiculous. But if it were picked . . . she did not want to think about what might happen if that woody, furrowed stem were cut, that thick dark orange rind cracked open.

The days passed, and October came, and soon most of the crop had been shipped, the balance put away in the storage shed, and Manuel and the other laborers were gone. All that remained in the fields were the dwarfs and the damaged and withered fruit that had been left to decay into natural fertilizer for the spring planting. And the strange pumpkin near the east fence, hidden under its thick plastic shroud.

Amanda was too busy, as always at harvesttime, to think much about the pumpkin. But she did go up there twice, once with Harley and once alone. The first time, Harley wanted to take off the sheeting and look at the thing; she wouldn't let him. The second time, alone, she had stood in a cold sea wind and felt again the emanation of evil, the responsive stirrings of terror and disgust. It was as if the pumpkin were trying to exert some telepathic force upon her, as if it were saying, "Cut my stem . . . open me up . . . eat me . . ." She pulled away finally, almost with a sense of having wrenched loose from grasping hands, and drove away determined to do something drastic: take a can of gasoline up there and set fire to the thing, burn it to a cinder, get *rid* of it once and for all.

But she didn't do it. When she got back to the house she had calmed down and her fears again seemed silly, childish. A telepathic pumpkin, for heaven's sake! A telepathic evil pumpkin! She didn't even tell Harley of the incident.

More days passed, most of October fell away like dry leaves, and the weekend before Halloween arrived—the weekend of the Pumpkin Festival. The crowds were thick on both Saturday and Sunday; Amanda, working the traditional Sutter Farm booth, sold dozens of pumpkins, mainly to families with children who wanted them for Halloween jack-o'-lanterns. She enjoyed herself the first day, but not the second. Harley entered his prize exhibition pumpkin in the annual contest—it had weighed out finally at 248 pounds—and fully expected to win his long-awaited second blue ribbon. And didn't. Aaron Douglas, who owned a farm up near Princeton, won first prize with a 260-pound Connecticut Field giant.

Harley took the loss hard. He wouldn't eat his supper Sunday night and moped around on Monday and Halloween Tuesday, spending most of both days at the stand they always set up near Highway One to catch any last-minute shoppers. There were several this year: everyone, it seemed, wanted a nice fat pumpkin for Halloween.

All Hallows' Eve.

Amanda stood at the kitchen window, looking out toward the fields. It was just after five o'clock, with night settling rapidly; a low wispy fog had come in off the Pacific and was curling around the outbuildings, hiding most of the land beyond. She could barely see the barn, where Harley had gone to his workshop. She wished he would come back, even if he was still broody over the results of the contest. It was quiet here in the house, a little too quiet to suit her, and she felt oddly restless.

Behind her on the stove, hard cider flavored with cinnamon bubbled in a big iron pot. Harley loved hot cider at this time of year; he'd had three cups before going out and it had flushed his face, put a faint slur in his voice—he never had been much of a drinking man. But she didn't mind. Alcohol loosened him up a bit, stripped away some of his reserve. Usually it made him laugh, too, but not tonight.

The fog seemed to be thickening; the lights in the barn had been reduced to smeary yellow blobs on the gray backdrop. A fine night for Halloween, she thought. And she smiled a wistful smile as a pang of nostalgia seized her.

Halloween had been a special night when she was a child, a night of exciting ritual. First, the carving of the jack-o'-lantern—how she'd loved that! Her father always brought home the biggest, roundest pumpkin he could find, and they would scoop it out together, and cut out its eyes and nose and jagged gap-toothed grin, and light the candle inside, and then set it grinning and glowing on the porch for all the neighbors to see. Then the dressing up in the costume her mother had made for her: a witch with a blacked-out front tooth and a tall-crowned hat, an old broom tucked under one arm; a ghost dressed in a sewn white sheet, her face smeared with cold cream; a lady pirate in a crimson tunic and an eye patch, carrying a wooden sword covered in tinfoil. Then the trick-or-treating, and the bags full of candy and gum and fruit and popcorn balls and caramel apples, and the harmless pranks like soaping old Mrs. Collier's windows because she never answered her doorbell, or tying bells to the tail of Mr. Dawson's cat. Then the party afterward, with all her friends from school—cake with Halloween icing and pumpkin pie, blindfold games and bobbing for apples, and afterward, with the lights turned out and the curtains open so they could see the jack-o'-lantern grinning and glowing on the porch, the ghost and goblin stories, and the delicious thrill of terror when her father described the fearful things that prowled and hunted on Hallowmas Eve.

Amanda's smile faded as she remembered that part of the ritual. Her father telling her that Halloween had originated among the ancient Druids, who believed that on this night, legions of evil spirits were called forth by the Lord of the Dead. Saying that the only way to ward them off was to light great fires, and even then . . . even then . . . Saying that on All Hallows' Eve, according to the ancient beliefs, evil was at its strongest and most profound.

Evil like that pumpkin out there?

She shuddered involuntarily and tried to peer past the shimmery outlines of the barn. But the east field was invisible now, clamped inside the bony grasp of the fog. That damned pumpkin! she thought. I *should* have taken some gasoline out there and set fire to it. Exorcism by fire.

Then she thought: Come on, Mandy, that's superstitious nonsense, just like Harley says. The pumpkin is just a pumpkin. Nothing is going to happen here tonight.

But it was so quiet . . .

Abruptly she turned from the window, went to the stove, and picked up her spoon; stirred the hot cider. If Harley didn't come back pretty soon, she'd put on her coat and go out to the workshop and fetch him. She just didn't like being here alone, not tonight of all nights.

So *quiet* . . .

The back door burst open.

She had no warning; the door flew inward, the knob thudding into the kitchen wall, and she cried out the instant she saw him standing there. "Harley! For God's sake, you half scared me to death! What's the idea of—"

Then she saw his face. And what he held dripping in his hand.

She screamed.

He came toward her, and she tried to run, and he caught her and threw her to the floor, pinned her there with his weight. His face loomed above her, stained with stringy pulp and seeds, and she knew what the cider and his brooding had led him to do tonight—knew what was about to happen even before the thing that had been Harley opened its goblin's mouth and the words came out in a drooling litany of evil.

"You're next . . . you're next . . . you're next . . . ."

The handful of dripping rind and pulp mashed against her mouth as she tried again to scream, forcing some of the bitter juice past her lips. She gagged, fought wildly for a few seconds . . . and then stopped struggling, lay still.

She smiled up at him, a wet dark orange smile.

Now there were two of them, the first two—two to sow the seeds for next year's Halloween harvest.

Introduction:

Lover in the Wildwood

BY FRANK BELKNAP LONG

Frank Belknap Long published his first short story in 1924, and for many years was among the most frequent and most popular contributors to *Weird Tales* and other magazines. Collections of his stories include *The Hounds of Tindalos, The Rim of the Unknown,* and *The Early Long.* Those stories not only helped to form the tastes of a generation of readers, they contributed to shaping a popular literary movement that has become a part of the American mainstream. It seems fair to say that every other writer in *Halloween Horrors* has been, in one way or another, influenced by Frank Belknap Long.

Since his youth, Long has been a poet. *The Goblin Tower* contains some of his best-known work in this field and displays his unerring use of language for emotional impact, his love affair with love itself, and a passion that continues to burn bright.

It is a special pleasure to present "Lover in the Wildwood," a new fantasy from Long's pen that manages to be, at the same time, both dark as night and bright as love.

Lover in the Wildwood

BY FRANK BELKNAP LONG

"Help me!" Katherine Oakley pleaded, leaning sharply forward in her wheelchair and shaking it with the intensity of her emotion. "On this night of all nights my beloved is waiting in the woods for me to come to him. We must go immediately, as you once promised."

Although compassion was close to the top of Helen Margrave's scale of values, bending hospital rules for a mental ward patient—just the thought of it—was making her realize how agonizing a certain kind of decision-making could be. That it might lead to her transference to another ward was of less concern to her than the simple fact that another nurse, under such circumstances, would almost certainly be a flint-hearted disciplinarian, with a disdain for any kind of innovative therapy.

Kathy was so old, frail, and pathetically withered-looking, so desperately in need of a change, however brief. Simply a chance to look up at the stars and feel for a short while free of all constraint, conditional and guarded as that freedom would have to be. How could the night wind caressing her cheeks and the fragrance of the flowers in an autumn that was still almost summerlike fail to have a soothing effect? And how could anyone who did not possess a heart of stone turn a deaf ear to a request so easy to grant?

They would be gone for less than an hour, and if something went wrong Dr. Richards would be the first to come to her defense, in long strides and with a smiling face. "Of course, of course," she could almost hear him saying. "You were impulsive, unthinking. But aren't we all guilty of being a little foolish at times? Total dedication is the important thing . . ."

Just the fact that she had ceased to be indecisive must have been mirrored in her expression, for Kathy's almost skeleton-thin fingers had gone out to fasten on her wrist and the wheelchair stopped shaking.

"First it was Aunt Margaret and then my brother, for fifteen long years, and now you," she said. "I feel ashamed to be so much in need of help. When I meet my beloved there is nothing but joy. At that moment all else is forgotten. It is selfish of me and of him too, I suppose. But just the rapture of our meeting, of our mingling—"

She stopped, as if she felt she had said enough. But when Helen remained silent she went on quickly, "My brother believed me, I had his trust. I must have yours. You nod, but why have you not said so?"

"Oh, I do believe you, Kathy," Helen said, upbraiding herself for the slowness of her response. "On All Hallows' Eve many spirits walk, and not all of them are Satan-spawned. It has been said that Saints walk too, without waiting for the evil ones to vanish at the first faint flush of dawn, if only because widows and orphans must be accorded protection when the Fiery Gates swing wide. And great and noble lovers, cut off from fulfillment in their prime . . ."

There seemed to be no need for her to go on, for Kathy had become calm again, so much so that for a moment she had seemed almost mesmerized. It was amazing how little guilt one could feel about lying when it was accompanied by a total forgetfulness of self. What surprised Helen just as much was how effortlessly the words had seemed to flow from her lips, since the last and only time she could recall having talked in that way had been at the bedside of her sister's five-year-old son during a "witching hour" reading of the old English nursery rhymes.

The problem was, to prove her sincerity to Kathy, Helen found it was necessary at times to treat her as a child and to appear to embrace her beliefs as if they were her own.

What perhaps she had always prided herself on most was her ability to act swiftly and decisively, once her doubts had been resolved, and she did so now.

She took firm hold of the wheelchair and started moving it across the hospital room, saying only, "It has always been a great wonder to me that you know the exact time of his appearance, to the hour—the exact minute, in fact—across the years. And although the location changes, the woods remain the same to you. Has it always been so?"

"Yes, always," Kathy said, staring about the bare walls as if the other's words had made her feel they might at any moment dissolve into a many-flowered garden of delight.

"It will take us only seven or eight minutes to get to the woods," Helen said. "So there is no great need to hurry. But I'll feel happier when we're outside the hospital, with the corridor risk behind us. That risk will increase if you talk at all. Do you understand how important silence is?"

"Oh, I do, I do," Kathy said. "I would kneel if I could and kiss your feet for what you are doing for me."

"There is no need for you to do anything so foolish," Helen assured her. "Just stay quiet and say nothing if we meet anyone. I don't think we will, for the passage we are taking is reserved for special nurses at this hour. No one is stationed there."

Pausing for an instant to press her charge's shoulder in reassurance—she had no respect for nurses who ignored such things—she wheeled her out into a corridor that was, at the moment, so hushed they could have heard the flickering of a candle inside a pumpkin, if one had been set down on the floor at the far end.

Into a narrower corridor they passed, and down a short ramp to a passageway so narrow it was hard to get the chair through without scraping the walls. Two minutes later they were outside the hospital, having emerged on the paved road which separated the building from the stretch of woodland just beyond.

The early evening balminess was almost unbelievably springlike, despite the October chill which had preceded it a week earlier, and down the road came three little girls, clearly heading for the row of apartment buildings that flanked the hospital on its eastern side.

They were quickly surrounded by the costumed juveniles, each with a wicker basket extended, their skull-faces swaying to and fro, their long, borrowed-from-mother robes trailing in the dust at the edge of the road.

"Trick-or-treat, trick-or-treat!" they piped in treble voices, crowding closer when they saw that Kathy was clutching what appeared to be a purse, although it was only a heavy handkerchief folded over.

"Please scatter, kiddies," Helen said, as gently as she could. "We just came out for a breath of fresh air, and there's nothing we can give you. But with costumes as scary as that you'll get more treats than you can carry."

"Children that age should not go roaming around after dark, pretending to be what they are not," Kathy said, as the costumed trio continued on down the roadway.

Helen found herself wondering, as they crossed the roadway and came within a few yards of the woods, whether or not, in her disturbed imaginings, Kathy had any real understanding of the brighter aspects of Halloween—its lighthearted merriment, masquerades, fortune telling, and fruit-dunking games.

Despite their hospital room conversations, those aspects could have been nebulous to her, since they were so overshadowed, in her disturbed mind, by the darker ones.

Helen even began to experience a little of that overshadowing herself as she looked up at the great trees—oaks and pines and cedars—grouped in patterns that seemed in some strange way made for this night, as if some invisible presence had rearranged them to cast the most somber and ghost-haunted of spells.

"It is not far to where my beloved waits," Kathy said. "I will tell you where we must stop."

That it proved to be a clearing came as no surprise, but Helen had hardly expected they would emerge so soon into one drenched with long shafts of moonlight streaming down between the trees, and with little pools of sky-mirroring water scattered about. It seemed in all respects an enchanted spot.

"I must be alone when he appears," Kathy said. "But you may remain near. Aunt Margaret and my brother always did. It is not sinful to watch such a great love unfold, for our reunion is always flamelike and immortal and aureoled in grace."

For a long moment silence reigned in the clearing and Helen went back in her mind to what she had considered from the first. In all likelihood, Kathy's delusion would be of brief duration. She would not be harmed by it, and when it passed she would feel, if only for a short while, fulfilled and at peace. Or at least, as much at peace as a mental ward patient could hope to be.

Did not such a likelihood demand some risk taking, even risking one's job, on the part of everyone to whom her care had been entrusted? Others, unfortunately, did not always see it that way, and she could respect and understand their opposition to any kind of unorthodox therapy. But to her the obligation was plain and she had no intention of evading it.

Kathy had straightened and begun to tremble a little and it seemed the right time to move from beside the wheelchair to the opposite side of the clearing. Her request to be alone was so understandable it seemed a little surprising that she had failed to repeat it.

It probably meant, Helen told herself as she turned about to look back at her, that the imaginary lover had not as yet made his appearance.

The light increased so slowly in brightness where Kathy was sitting that for a long moment there seemed to be nothing unusual about it. Woodland vistas had a way of growing darker and brighter by turns as slight gusts of wind stirred the foliage, or a cloud wisp passed fleetingly across the face of the moon. Then, abruptly, it blazed all about her, in a dazzle so great it flooded all the aisles of the woods, and though the wheelchair remained stationary, it seemed, for an instant, to have been turned into a small chariot of fire.

The figure emerged almost as abruptly, tall and straight and clad in a seamless garment the color of the autumn woods. The garment was short, but slightly flowing, and loosely belted at the waist, and so nondescript it could have been worn by a shepherd in ancient Greece, or in one of the mountain villages of the Middle Ages, or even in the Spain or Italy of today. But there was nothing nondescript about the masculine strength and great beauty of the face that looked down on Kathy, who was rising in the chair with a glad cry.

It happened all at once and very quickly. The garment had left the figure's arms and shoulders bare, and his arms reached out, lifted Kathy from the chair, and folded her into his embrace.

For an instant all that Helen could see outside of the figure's tightening arms was Kathy's long, unbound hair streaming downward from her waist. But there are no caresses, however impassioned or prolonged, in which relaxation plays no part, and in a momentary pause before they were resumed again, Helen saw a Kathy transfigured, transformed.

There are several kinds of loveliness and Kathy's face and figure seemed, in some miraculous way, to possess them all. If, in her flawless complexion, ecstasy-parted lips, and lustrous dark eyes, she bore the look of an entranced schoolgirl experiencing love's awakening for the first time, she seemed even more to resemble, in other ways, some halo-wearing goddess of the ancient world whose secret amorousness had provoked Olympian wars.

It was then that the feeling swept over Helen that she had, for the barest instant, been caught up in the spell in a way that made her more than an onlooker, that the figure knew she was standing there watching. More than watching. Feeling, in the inmost core of her being, his lips pressed to hers, his strong hands moving up and down and across her back. For the briefest of moments he raised his head, and their eyes met.

Then, in a blaze of light that matched the one which had accompanied his arrival, the figure was gone and Kathy was back in the wheelchair.

The shaking began then and would not stop. It lasted for a full minute, making it impossible for her to move. It was almost impossible for her to believe and yet—and yet— How could she doubt what she had seen? Through some unheard-of dislodgement of space and time she had watched an old woman's youth restored.

Other thoughts, just as unsettling, had come crowding in upon her mind, threatening the reality of beliefs she had held from childhood, but she put them from her as she went stumbling back across the clearing. The violent shaking had left her, but so much unsteadiness remained that she caught her heel in a tangle of vines and almost went sprawling before she reached the wheelchair.

"Kathy, Kathy, are you all right?" were the first words she spoke to the chair's slumped occupant—and the last.

Death can announce its presence in many ways, but even to a nurse, who has still the need of making absolutely sure, the utter stillness of sagging and aging flesh can be a potent doubt-dispeller.

Twenty minutes later Helen was back in the hospital room, her brief absence unsuspected, talking to Dr. Richards on the bedside phone.

"Yes," she said. "She was just starting to get out of the wheelchair when she fell forward and collapsed in my arms. I got her back into the chair. Yes, of course. I knew at once she was gone, but of course I've made sure. Her heart . . ."

The moon had broken through a heavy overcast and was shining brightly when Helen crossed the paved road in front of the hospital. She found herself almost running.

Another year, another year, she thought. How quickly time sweeps past when you must administer to the needs of your patients, the poor souls entrusted to your care, and try, so very hard, to make their needs your own.

Ah, Kathy—how little you knew or even suspected we shared the same kind of struggle, the same needs and wild desires, handicapped as I was by what the world calls sanity. The instant I met his eyes I saw that he knew also. From death he could not save you, Kathy. No one can be spared the descent of that great and terrible scythe.

It was the last time for you, Kathy—the very last time after many long years. He knew, though I did not. You were so ailing, it was his last goodbye. He could keep you young and radiant. Forever, yes, but "forever" has no meaning when it is time for the scythe to descend. One night in the year can be forever, but not when Death comes reaping. And it is "forever" in this world that we seek and cherish, Kathy. Beyond that—nothing is known.

I am still young, Kathy, and men find me attractive. I may have more than one marriage. But just to know that there is one for whom I shall never age and be forever beautiful—if only for one night in the year—yes, Kathy, yes. That is why I am hurrying now.

Remember what the poet wrote—the poet who was perhaps the greatest of the great? "Forever wilt thou love, and she be fair." I have changed it a little, Kathy, a sacrilege with a line so great, but no matter. "Always will he love and *I* be fair." No, even more, a greater sacrilege, for it breaks the rhythm. "Always will he love and *keep* me fair."

I know now, just as you did, Kathy—the exact hour, the exact minute, on this night of all nights, when I shall be in my beloved's arms.

Introduction:

Apples

BY RAMSEY CAMPBELL

Ramsey Campbell sold his first short story to August Derleth in 1962 when he was sixteen. *The Inhabitant of the Lake,* his first collection of stories, was published two years later. Subsequent collections include *Demons by Daylight, The Height of the Scream,* and *Dark Companions.* He has also edited several successful anthologies, including *New Terrors, New Tales of the Cthulhu Mythos,* and a pleasant volume of unpleasantries for children called *The Gruesome Book.* In recent years, he has given most of his time to novels; they include *The Doll Who Ate His Mother, The Face That Must Die, The Parasite, The Nameless,* and *Incarnate.*

Reviewing *Dark Companions* in the Washington *Post* in 1982, I wrote that "in Campbell's very modern world, things are bad to begin with . . . and then they get worse."

Remember, as you read his story here, that apples can be tart as well as sweet.

Apples

BY RAMSEY CAMPBELL

We wanted to be scared on Halloween, but not like that. We never meant anything to happen to Andrew. We only wanted him not to be so useless and show us he could do something he was scared of doing. I know I was scared the night I went to the allotments when Mr. Gray was still alive.

We used to watch him from Colin's window in the tenements, me and Andrew and Colin and Colin's little sister, Jill. Sometimes he worked in his allotment until midnight, my mum once said. The big lamps on the paths through the estate made his face look like a big white candle with a long nose that was melting. Jill kept shouting "Mr. Toad" and shutting the window quick, but he never looked up. Only he must have known it was us and that's why he said we took his apples when kids from the other end of the estate did really.

He took our mums and dads to see how they'd broken his hedge because he'd locked his gate. "If Harry says he didn't do it, then he didn't," my dad said and Colin's, who was a wrestler, said, "If I find out who's been up to no good they'll be walking funny for a while." But Andrew's mum only said, "I just hope you weren't mixed up in this, Andrew." His dad and mum were like that, they were teachers and tried to make him friends at our school they taught at, boys who didn't like getting dirty and always had combs and handkerchiefs. So then whenever we were cycling round the paths by the allotments and Mr. Gray saw us he said things like, "There are the children who can't keep their hands off other people's property," to anyone who was passing. So one night Colin pinched four apples off his tree, and then it was my turn.

I had to wait for a night my mum sent me to the shop. The woman isn't supposed to sell kids cigarettes, but she does because she knows my mum. I came back past the allotments and when I got to Mr. Gray's I ducked down behind the hedge.

The lamps that were supposed to stop people being mugged turned everything grey in the allotments and made Mr. Gray's windows look as if they had metal shutters on. I could hear my heart jumping. I went to where the hedge was low and climbed over.

He'd put broken glass under the hedge. I managed to land on tiptoe in between the bits of glass. I hated him then, and I didn't even bother taking apples from where he mightn't notice, I just pulled some off and threw them over the hedge for the worms to eat. We wouldn't have eaten them, all his apples tasted old and bitter. I gave my mum her cigarettes and went up to Colin's and told Andrew, "Your turn next."

He started hugging himself. "I can't. My parents might know."

"They said we were stealing, as good as said it," Jill said. "They probably thought you were. My dad said he'd pull their heads off and stick them you-know-where if he thought that's what they meant about us."

"You've got to go," Colin said. "Harry went and he's not even eleven. Go now if you like before my mum and dad come back from the pub."

Andrew might have thought Colin meant to make him, because he started shaking and saying, "No I won't," and then there was a stain on the front of his trousers. "Look at the baby weeing himself," Colin and Jill said.

I felt sorry for him. "Maybe he doesn't feel well. He can go another night."

"I'll go if he won't," Jill said.

"You wouldn't let a girl go, would you?" Colin said to Andrew, but then their mum and dad came back. Andrew ran upstairs and Colin said to Jill, "You really would have gone too, wouldn't you?"

"I'm still going." She was so cross she went red. "I'm just as brave as you two, braver." And we couldn't stop her the next night, when her mum was watching Jill's dad at work being the Hooded Gouger.

I thought she'd be safe. There'd been a storm in the night and the wind could have blown down the apples. But I was scared when I saw how small she looked down there on the path under the lamps, and I'd never noticed how long it took to walk to the allotments, all that way she might have to run back. Her shadow kept disappearing as if something was squashing it and then it jumped in front of her. We couldn't see in Mr. Gray's windows for the lamps.

When she squatted down behind Mr. Gray's hedge, Andrew said, "Looks like she's been taken short," to try to sound like us, but Colin just glared at him. She threw her coat on the broken glass, then she got over the hedge and ran to the tree. The branches were too high for her. "Leave it," Colin said, but she couldn't have heard him, because she started climbing. She was halfway up when Mr. Gray came out of his house.

He'd got a pair of garden shears. He grinned when he saw Jill, because even all that far away we could see his teeth. He ran round to where the hedge was low. He couldn't really run, it was like a fat old white dog trying, but there wasn't anywhere else for Jill to climb the hedge. Colin ran out, and I was going to open the window and shout at Mr. Gray when he climbed over the hedge to get Jill.

He was clicking the shears. I could see the blades flash. Andrew wet himself and ran upstairs, and I couldn't open the window or even move. Jill jumped off the tree and hurt her ankles, and when she tried to get away from him she was nearly as slow as he was. But she ran to the gate and tried to climb it, only it fell over. Mr. Gray ran after her waving the shears when she tried to crawl away, and then he grabbed his chest like they do in films when they're shot, and fell into the hedge.

Colin ran to Jill and brought her back, and all that time Mr. Gray didn't move. Jill was shaking but she never cried, only shouted through the window at Mr. Gray. "That'll teach you," she shouted, even when Colin said, "I think he's dead." We were glad until we remembered Jill's coat was down there on the glass.

I went down though my chest was hurting. Mr. Gray was leaning over the hedge with his hands hanging down as if he was trying to reach the shears that had fallen standing up in the earth. His eyes were open with the lamps in them and looking straight at Jill's coat. He looked as if he'd gone bad somehow, as if he'd go all out of shape if you poked him. I grabbed Jill's coat, and just then the hedge creaked and he leaned forward as if he was trying to reach me. I ran away and didn't look back, because I was sure that even though he was leaning further his head was up so he could keep watching me.

I didn't sleep much that night and I don't think the others did. I kept getting up to see if he'd moved, because I kept thinking he was creeping up on the tenements. He was always still in the hedge, until I fell asleep, and when I looked again he wasn't there. The ambulance must have taken him away, but I couldn't get to sleep for thinking I could hear him on the stairs.

Next night my mum and dad were talking about how some woman found him dead in the hedge and the police went into his house. My mum said the police found a whole bedroom full of rotten fruit, and some books in his room about kids. Maybe he didn't like kids because he was afraid what he might do to them, she said, but that was all she'd say.

Colin and me dared each other to look in his windows and Jill went too. All we could see was rooms with nothing in them now except sunlight making them look dusty. I could smell rotten fruit and I kept thinking Mr. Gray was going to open one of the doors and show us his face gone bad. We went to see how many apples were left on his tree, only we didn't go in the allotment because when I looked at the house I saw a patch on one of the windows as if someone had wiped it clean to watch us. Jill said it hadn't been there before we'd gone to the hedge. We stayed away after that, and every night when I looked out of my room the patch was like a white face watching from his window.

Then someone else moved into his house and by the time the clocks went back and it got dark an hour earlier, we'd forgotten about Mr. Gray, at least Colin and Jill and me had. It was nearly Halloween and then a week to Guy Fawkes Night. Colin was going to get some zombie videos to watch on Halloween because his mum and dad would be at the wrestling, but then Andrew's mum found out. Andrew came and told us he was having a Halloween party instead. "If you don't come there won't be anyone," he said.

"All right, we'll come," Colin said, but Jill said, "Andrew's just too scared to watch the zombies. I expect they make him think of Mr. Toad. He's scared of Mr. Toad even now he's dead."

Andrew got red and stamped his foot. "You wait," he said.

The day before Halloween, I saw him hanging round near Mr. Gray's allotment when it was getting dark. He turned away when I saw him, pretending he wasn't there. Later I heard him go upstairs slowly as if he was carrying something, and I nearly ran out to catch him and make him go red.

I watched telly until my mum told me to go to bed three times. Andrew always went to bed as soon as his mum came home from night school. I went to draw my curtains and I saw someone in Mr. Gray's allotment, bending down under the apple tree as if he was looking for something. He was bending down so far I thought he was digging his face in the earth. When he got up his face looked too white under the lamps, except for his mouth that was messy and black. I pulled the curtains and jumped into bed in case he saw me, but I think he was looking at Andrew's window.

Next day at school Andrew bought Colin and Jill and me sweets. He must have been making sure we went to his party. "Where'd you get all that money?" Jill wanted to know.

"Mummy gave it to me to buy apples," Andrew said and started looking round as if he was scared someone could hear him.

He wouldn't walk home past Mr. Gray's. He didn't know I wasn't going very near after what I'd seen in the allotment. He went the long way round behind the tenements. I got worried when I didn't hear him come in and I went down in case some big kids had done him. He was hiding under the bonfire we'd all built behind the tenements for Guy Fawkes Night. He wouldn't tell me who he was hiding from. He nearly screamed when I looked in at him in the tunnel he'd made under there.

"Don't go if you don't want to," my mum said because I took so long over my tea. "I better had," I said, but I waited until Andrew came to find out if we were ever going, then we all went up together. It wasn't his party we minded so much as his mum and dad telling us what to do.

The first thing his dad said when we went in was "Wipe your feet," though we hadn't come from outside. It was only him there, because Andrew's mum was going to come back soon so he could go to a meeting. Then he started talking in the kind of voice teachers put on just before the holidays to make you forget they're teachers. "I expect your friends would like a Halloween treat," he said and got some baked potatoes out of the oven, but only Andrew had much. I'd just eaten and, besides, the smell of apples kept getting into the taste of the potatoes and making me feel funny.

There were apples hanging from a rope across the room and

floating in a washing-up bowl full of water on some towels on the floor. "If that's the best your friends can do with my Halloween cuisine I think it's about time for games," Andrew's dad said and took our plates away, grousing like a school dinner lady. When he came back, Andrew said, "Please may you tie my hands."

"I don't know about that, son." But Andrew gave him a handkerchief to tie them with and looked as if he was going to cry, so his dad said, "Hold them out, then."

"No, behind my back."

"I don't think your mother would permit that." Then he must have seen how Andrew wanted to be brave in front of us, so he made a face and tied them. "I hope your friends have handkerchiefs too," he said.

He tied our hands behind our backs, wrinkling his nose at Jill's handkerchief, and we let him for Andrew's sake. "Now the point of the game is to bring down an apple by biting it," he said, as if we couldn't see why the apples were hanging up. Only I wished he wouldn't go on about it because talking about them seemed to make the smell stronger.

Jill couldn't quite reach. When he held her up she kept bumping the apple with her nose and said a bad word when the apple came back and hit her. He put her down then quick and Colin had a go. His mouth was almost as big as one of the apples, and he took a bite first time, then he spat it out on the floor. "What on earth do you think you're doing? Would you do that at home?" Andrew's dad shouted, back to being a teacher again, and went to get a dustpan and a mop.

"Where did you get them apples?" Colin said to Andrew. Andrew looked at him to beg him not to ask in front of his dad, and we all knew. I remembered not noticing there weren't any apples on Mr. Gray's tree any more. We could see Andrew was trying to show us he wasn't scared, only he had to wait until his mum or dad was there. When his dad finished clearing up after Colin, Andrew said, "Let's have duck-apples now."

He knelt down by the bowl of water and leaned his head in. He kept his face in the water so long I thought he was looking at something and his dad went to him in case he couldn't get up. He pulled his face out spluttering and I went next, though I didn't like how nervous he looked now.

I wished I hadn't. The water smelled stale and tasted worse.

Whenever I tried to pick up an apple with just my mouth without biting into it, it sank and then bobbed up, and I couldn't see it properly. I didn't like not being able to see the bottom of the bowl. I had another go at an apple so I could get away, but Andrew's dad or someone must have stood over me, because the water got darker and I thought the apple bobbing up was bigger than my head and looking at me. I felt as if someone was holding my head down in the water and I couldn't breathe. I tried to knock the bowl over and spilled a bit of water on the towels. Andrew's dad hauled me out of the bowl as if I was a dog. "I think we'll dispense with the duck-apples," he said, and then the doorbell rang.

"That must be your mother without her keys again," he told Andrew, sounding relieved. "Just don't touch anything until one of us is here." He went down and we heard the door slam and then someone coming up. It wasn't him, the footsteps were too slow and loud. I kept tasting the appley water and feeling I was going to be sick. The footsteps took so long I thought I wouldn't be able to look when they came in. The door opened and Jill screamed, because there was someone wearing a dirty sheet and a skull for a face. "It's only Mummy," Andrew said, laughing at Jill for being scared. "She said she might dress up."

Just then the doorbell rang again and made us all jump. Andrew's mum closed the door of the flat as if the bell wasn't even ringing. "It must be children," Andrew said, looking proud of himself because he was talking for his mother. Jill was mad at him for laughing at her. "I want to duck for apples," she said, even though the smell was stronger and rottener. "I didn't have a go."

Andrew's mum nodded and went round making sure our hands were tied properly, then she pushed Jill to the bowl without taking her hands from under the sheet. Jill looked at her to tell her she didn't care if she wanted to pretend that much, Jill wasn't scared. The bell rang again for a long time but we all ignored it. Jill bent over the bowl and Andrew's mum leaned over her. The way she was leaning I thought she was going to hold Jill down, except Jill dodged out of the way. "There's something in there," she said.

"There's only apples," Andrew said. "I didn't think *you'd* be scared." Jill looked as if she'd have hit him if she'd been able to get her hands from behind her back. "I want to try the apples hanging up again," she said. "I didn't have a proper go."

She went under the rope and tried to jump high enough to get an apple, and then something tapped on the window. She nearly fell down, and even Colin looked scared. I know I was, because I thought someone had climbed up to the third floor to knock on the window. I thought Mr. Gray had. But Andrew grinned at us because his mum was there and said, "It's just those children again throwing stones."

His mum picked Jill up and Jill got the apple first time. She bit into it just as more stones hit the window, and then we heard Andrew's dad shouting outside. "It's me, Andrew. Let me in. Some damn fool locked me out when I went down."

Jill made a noise as if she was trying to scream. She'd spat out the apple and goggled at it on the floor. Something was squirming in it. I couldn't move and Colin couldn't either, because Andrew's mum's hands had come out from under the sheet to hold Jill. Only they were white and dirty, and they didn't look like any woman's hands. They didn't look much like hands at all.

Then both the arms came worming out from under the sheet to hold Jill so she couldn't move any more than Colin and me could, and the head started shaking to get the mask off. I'd have done anything rather than see underneath, the arms looked melted enough. All we could hear was the rubber mask creaking and something flopping round inside it, and the drip on the carpet from Andrew wetting himself. But suddenly Andrew squeaked, the best he could do for talking. "You leave her alone. She didn't take your apples, I did. You come and get me."

The mask slipped as if him under the sheet was putting his head on one side, then the arms dropped Jill and reached out for Andrew. Andrew ran to the door and we saw he'd got his hands free. He ran onto the stairs saying, "Come on, you fat old toad, try and catch me."

Him under the sheet went after him and we heard them running down, Andrew's footsteps and the others that sounded bare and squelchy. Me and Colin ran to Jill when we could move to see if she was all right apart from being sick on the carpet. When I saw she was, I ran down fast so that I wouldn't think about it, to find Andrew.

I heard his dad shouting at him behind the tenements. "Did you do this? What's got into you?" Andrew had got matches from somewhere and set light to the bonfire. His dad didn't see anything else, but I did, a sheet and something jumping about inside it, under all that fire. Andrew must have crawled through the tunnel he'd made but him in the sheet had got stuck. I watched the sheet flopping about when the flames got to it, then it stopped moving when the tunnel caved in on it. "Come upstairs, I want a few words with you," Andrew's dad said, pulling him by his ear. But when we got in the building he let go and just gaped, because Andrew's hair had gone dead white.

Introduction:

Pranks

BY ROBERT BLOCH

Robert Bloch has been heard to say that he'd prefer to be known as the man who wrote the Bible, rather than as the man who wrote *Psycho,* but that's not likely to happen. Since his first story was published in 1934, his writing has definitely tended toward the *unholy.* With his screenplays, novels—*The Scarf* and *American Gothic* are particularly notable, and his recent *The Night of the Ripper*—and many collections of stories, Bloch has long since proved himself an undisputed master of the macabre.

And nowhere is he more masterful—or more macabre, for that matter—than in the short story. Here are some Halloween pranks from a man who definitely did not write the Bible.

Pranks

BY ROBERT BLOCH

The lights came on just after sunset.

He stood in the hallway, near the front door, filling the candy dish on the table with a skill born of long practice. How many times had he done this, how many Halloweens had he spent preparing for the joyful hours of the evening ahead? No use trying to remember; he'd lost count. Not that it mattered, really. What mattered was the occasion itself, the few hours of magic and make-believe one was privileged to share with the children. What mattered was the opportunity, however brief, to enter into the spirit of things, participate in the let's-pretend on the one night of the year when a childless couple could themselves pretend that they were truly no different from the members of the community around them; solid, ordinary citizens who took pride in their homes and their offspring.

Actually it wasn't all pretense; he was proud of this house, and rightly so, for it was he who had designed and created it, right down to the last knickknack and stick of furniture. And they had always loved children.

But truth to tell, it was the make-believe that thrilled him. Maybe they both had a childish streak of their own, dressing up to surprise the youngsters. And part of the fun was surprising one another, for it was an unspoken rule that neither of them ever revealed in advance just what sort of costume they'd be wearing.

Now, hearing her footsteps on the stairs, his eyes brightened in eager anticipation. One year she'd come sailing down the steps in hoopskirts as Scarlett O'Hara, another time she'd gotten herself up as a black-braided Pocahontas, once she'd worn the powdered wig of a Marie Antoinette. What would he see tonight—Cleopatra, the Empress Josephine, Joan of Arc?

Leave it to her to fathom his expectations and astonish him with the unexpected. And that, as she descended into full view, was exactly what she did. For instead of a figure out of film or fiction he beheld a little old lady with a motherly smile, wearing an apron over a simple housedress, as though she had just stepped out of an old-fashioned country kitchen.

"How do you like it?" she said.

For a moment he stared at her, completely taken aback, yet puzzled by the odd familiarity of her appearance. Where had he seen this smiling elderly woman before? Then, suddenly, his gaze darted toward the candy dish on the table and the empty box beside it. And there on the front of the box was his answer—the oval photographic portrait purporting to represent the candy-maker herself. Tonight she was Mrs. See.

Now it was his turn to smile. "Marvelous!" he said. "It's hard for me to imagine you as an old lady, but I must say you look the part."

She nodded, pleased with his reaction. "I think the kids will like it. And they certainly should be able to recognize you too, Ben."

He peered at her through the tiny rimless spectacles and patted his paunch. "I hope so. At least I make a better Ben Franklin than last year's Abraham Lincoln. Though I admit I was tempted to try something different for a change. Remember when I did Adolf Hitler—"

"And scared half the children out of their wits?" She shook her head. "Halloween's for fun, not fright. No, I think you made a good choice."

She bustled over to the table, inspecting the mound of chocolates heaped on the candy dish. "I see you've done my job for me."

"That's right." He paused, listening to the sudden chiming of the grandfather's clock beside the stairs. "Half past seven. They should start coming soon."

Then the doorbell rang.

She opened the door and the two of them stood side by side, gazing down at the little ragamuffin in the cowboy outfit as he clutched his crumpled shopping bag and rattled off the time-honored greeting. "Trick-or-treat," he said.

She stepped back, smiling. "Isn't he adorable?" she murmured. Then, "Come right in and help yourself. The candy's on the table."

The moment the front door closed, Joe Stuttman turned to Maggie, scowling. "Jesus H. Christ!" he said.

"Now, Joe, please!" Maggie sighed. "Don't get yourself upset over nothing."

"You call that nothing?" His scowl and voice deepened. "Those damned costumes must have cost a fortune. I'm not blind, you know—I read the ads. Okay, so most of Angela's witch outfit you made yourself, but why in hell you had to go and buy Robbie that fancy space suit—"

"Simmer down," Maggie told him. "You don't have to pay for it. I've been saving up from my household allowance these past two months."

"So that's it!" Joe shook his head. "No wonder we've been eating so many of those lousy casserole messes lately. I work my tail off down at the shop and all I get to eat is glob because your son has to dress up like a goddamn astronaut for Halloween!"

"Our son," Maggie said softly. "Robbie's a good boy. You saw his last report card—all those A's mean he's really been doing his homework. And he still finds time to help me around the house and do your yard work for you. I think he deserves a treat once in a while."

"Treat." Joe went over to the coffee table in front of the television set, picked up the six-pack resting there, then yanked out a can of beer. "That's another thing I don't like—this trick-or-treat business. Running up and down the street at night, knocking on doors and asking for a handout. I don't care what kind of a fancy getup a kid's wearing. What's he's really doing is acting like some wino on Main Street, a bum mooching off strangers. You call that good behavior? It's nothing but blackmail if you ask me." He thumbed the beer can tab. "Trick-or-treat—it's a threat, isn't it? Pay up or else. What are you training Robbie for, to grow up and join the Mafia?"

"For heaven's sake," Maggie said. "You don't have to go on a roll about it. You know as well as I do that trick-or-treat is just a phrase. People expect kids to ask them for candy or cookies on Halloween, it's just a tradition, that's all. And if somebody doesn't come through with a treat I'm sure neither Robbie nor Angela is going to do anything about it. They'll just go on to another house." She glanced unhappily toward the front door. "I only wish you'd let me put out a few little goodies for the kids who come here."

"No way," Joe said. He took a gulp of beer. "I thought we had that all settled. I'm not wasting my money on a mess of junk food for a bunch of little bastards who dress up in stupid costumes and come banging on my front door."

"But, Joe—"

"You heard me." Joe scooped up the six-pack with his free hand. "Now let's get those lights turned off, quick, before anyone shows up. I'm gonna watch the game on the set in the bedroom, and I don't want any interruptions. That means don't answer the door, do you read me?"

"Yes," Maggie said. "I read you."

Wearily she turned and started down the hallway toward the kitchen as Joe turned the living room lamp off behind her.

Do you read me? What a stupid question! Of course Maggie could read Joe, she'd been reading him like a book these past twelve years. And there were no surprises awaiting her; the stinginess, the rages, the insensitivity to the needs of others, all were part of an old, old story she'd come to know only too well.

Sighing softly, Maggie began to stack the dishes in the sink. As she did so she reminded herself that she had to be fair. Joe did work awfully hard, he did try to protect his family, and as husbands went he was probably better than most. In spite of his faults, Joe was a good man.

And maybe that was the trouble—he was a good man. A man who seemed never to have enjoyed his childhood, and who couldn't share in the fun his own children wanted to enjoy.

So it was up to her to see that they had a little of that fun in their lives. Like tonight—Halloween—a fun time for kids like Robbie and Angela. She hoped they were having a good time; perhaps when they grew up with families of their own they'd still be able to enjoy a harmless holiday.

It seemed to take forever for the twins to get ready; Pam's devil costume was too tight and had to be let out at the waist before it could be zipped up in back, and Debbie kept fussing with her clown makeup.

In point of fact, they didn't actually leave the house until almost eight-fifteen, but within three minutes after their departure Chuck and Linda Cooper were in bed.

"Alone at last!" Linda giggled. "My God, you'd think I was some kind of floozy, sneaking around like this and waiting for a chance to hop into the sack the moment the coast is clear."

"Be a floozy," Chuck said. "Come on, I dare you."

"Don't get me wrong." Linda sobered. "You know how much I love the kids, we both do. But lately it seems like we never get a chance, what with their bedroom right next door to ours and these damned mattress springs squeaking. I'm always afraid they can hear us."

"So let them hear." Chuck grinned. "About time they learned the facts of life."

Linda shook her head. "But they're still so young! Maybe I'm too self-conscious, I don't know. It's the way I was brought up, I guess, and I can't help it."

"Look, let's not talk about it now, shall we?" Chuck tossed the covers aside. "I'm not going to spend the next two hours worrying whether or not the bedsprings squeak."

"Sorry," Linda said. "I know how tight things are right now, the way prices keep going up and you not getting that raise until next year. But if we could only afford a new mattress—"

"Buy you one for Christmas. How's about that?"

"Oh, Chuck!" She turned to him, smiling. "Do you really mean it?"

"Course I mean it. One new mattress for Christmas, that's a promise. But right now we've got another holiday to celebrate, remember?" He took her into his arms. "Happy Halloween," he said.

Sometime around nine-thirty Father Carmichael checked his watch. "Getting late," he said. "I really should be going. I thank you both for a lovely dinner and a delightful evening—"

"Come on, Father, what's your hurry?" Jim Higgins reached for the bottle and leaned forward to pour a good two inches of its contents into the priest's brandy snifter. "One for the road, okay?" he said.

Father Carmichael shrugged in mild protest, but Martha Higgins beamed and nodded at him from her chair beside the fireplace. "Please don't rush away. Billy and Pat should be home soon and I know they'd love to see you."

"I'd like that." The priest twirled his snifter, then raised it to drink, smiling as he did so. Then, as he set the glass down again, his expression changed. "Aren't they a little young to be out at this hour?"

"It's trick-or-treat night, don't you remember?" Jim Higgins swallowed brandy in a single swig that emptied his own snifter. "After all, Halloween only comes once a year."

"Praise the Lord for that," Father Carmichael said softly.

Martha Higgins raised her eyebrows. "Don't you approve of trick-or-treat?"

"A harmless diversion," the priest told her. "But Halloween itself—"

"Now wait a minute." Jim Higgins spoke quickly, glancing at Martha out of the corner of his eye as he did so. "This is a nice friendly little town. You of all people should know that, Father. I realize a lot of parents go along with their youngsters on a night like this, but we talked it over and decided it was time for Billy and Pat to make the rounds alone if they wanted to. Sort of gives them a grown-up feeling, and helps them to understand there's nothing to be afraid of."

"Nothing to be afraid of." The priest sighed. Then, conscious of Martha Higgins' sudden frown, he forced a smile. "Don't mind me," he said. "It's the brandy talking."

"What do you mean?" Jim Higgins was frowning too. "What's all this about Halloween? Are you trying to tell us we ought to be afraid of goblins and witches? I thought people stopped believing in that stuff a couple of hundred years ago."

"So they did." Father Carmichael took a hasty sip from his glass. "They stopped believing. But that in itself didn't necessarily stop the phenomena."

"Don't talk like a damned fool!" Jim Higgins said, then halted, his face reddening. "Sorry, Father—no offense—"

"And none taken." The priest nodded. "You're quite right, of course. We're all of us God's fools, and some of us, I fear, are damned. But I spoke as neither, merely in my capacity as a servant of the Church. And though the Church no longer concerns itself with suppressing old wives' tales about pixies and leprechauns, it has not abandoned the fight against true evil. There are still those of us who are ordained to seek out and dispel the unclean and the unholy, or exorcise unfortunates possessed by demons."

"But isn't a lot of that just superstition?" Martha said. "All this nonsense about vampires and werewolves and the dead coming out of their graves? And even if such things were possible, I don't see what it has to do with Halloween. It's just another holiday."

Father Carmichael finished his brandy before speaking. "The real holiday—holy day, that is—will come tomorrow, on the Feast of All Saints. It's then we celebrate Hallowmass in honor of Our Lady and all the martyrs unknown who died to preserve the faith. The faith which Satan abhors, because it affirms the power of Almighty God.

"But Satan too has power. And he chooses to manifest his defiance on the eve of Allhallows by loosing the forces of evil which he commands." The priest broke off, smiling self-consciously. "Forgive me—I didn't mean to start preaching a sermon. And I hope you realize I was just speaking figuratively, so to say."

"Sure thing." Jim Higgins moved to his wife and put his hand on her shoulder. "Just a little Halloween ghost story, right?"

Martha nodded but her eyes were troubled, intent on Father Carmichael as he glanced at his watch again, then rose.

"Time I was leaving," he said. "I take it I'll be seeing you both at Mass tomorrow—"

Martha gestured quickly. "But you haven't seen the children yet! They should be here any minute now. Please, Father. Won't you stay?"

The priest hesitated, conscious that the smile had faded from her face as he stared into the troubled eyes.

"Of course," he said. "Of course I'll stay."

Then there was silence, except for the crackle of flames in the fireplace and the faint, faraway ticking of a clock.

Jim Higgins frowned. "Almost ten-thirty," he murmured. "They promised to be back by ten at the latest." The frown deepened. "You'll pardon my language, Father—but where in hell are those kids?"

"Heavely," Irene Esterhazy said. "I mean heavenly." She lurched against the buffet table as she took another bite of her croissant. "Try one, honey—they're soooo good!"

Howard Esterhazy shook his head. "No time for that," he told her. "We've stayed too long as it is."

"But it's such a lovely party." Irene turned, nodding toward the crowd of couples milling about in the living room beyond, her voice rising above the babble of animated conversation. "Besides, I want 'nother drink—"

She lurched again and Howard gripped her shoulder. "You've had enough," he said. "We're going home."

"Oh, Howie—"

"You heard me." He guided her forward. "Now pull yourself together and say good night to our host and hostess."

Irene made a face. "Must I?"

"You must," Howard said.

And she did, somehow managing not to slur her words as they exchanged farewells and made their way out to the driveway.

Once in the car, with the windows open and the night air fanning her face, Irene sobered slightly. "You mad at me, honey?"

"No." Howard sighed, eyes intent on the road. "I guess you're entitled to a little diversion once in a while. But do you realize what time it is?"

Irene focused her eyes on the illuminated dial of the dashboard clock. "My God, you're right! It's almost eleven. I had no idea—"

Her husband nodded. "I know. And I didn't want to spoil your fun. It's just that I told Connie we wouldn't be late."

"Maybe we ought to give her a little something extra," Irene said. "She's always been so good about sitting with Mark, even though she does play that damn stereo full blast."

"You can say that again," Howard muttered as they pulled up before the house. The wind was rising, sending surges of sound through the treetops, but the screech of the stereo echoed so loudly that even their voices were drowned by its pounding beat as they left the car and moved up to the front door.

Howard's thumb jabbed at the buzzer. "Maybe I should use the key," he said. "She can't hear anything over that racket."

But as he fumbled in his pocket the door swung open quickly and Connie peered out. "Oh, it's you—" she said.

"Who did you expect, Michael Jackson?" Howard scowled.

"I thought it was Mark." Connie's voice faltered.

"Mark?" Irene moved into the hall, her forehead furrowing. "You mean he isn't here?"

"Please, Mrs. Esterhazy." The girl gestured helplessly. "Don't be angry with me. I thought it would be all right." Her voice was muffled by stereophonic stridency.

"Turn that thing off!" Howard shouted.

Retreating to the living room, Connie hastily obeyed, then turned to confront the Esterhazys' accusing stare.

"Now what's all this about Mark?" Howard said. "Where is he?"

Connie's gaze dropped and her words came with forced bravado. "You know Bill Summers, that friend of his from down the street? Well, he came to the door and I thought it was trick-or-treat, but it turned out he wanted Mark to come out with him. Just around the block, he said, because he didn't want to go alone. I told Mark no, he wasn't supposed to, and he had all the candy he wanted right here at home that you left for him. Besides, he didn't even have a costume. But Bill said it would only be for a few minutes, and Mark was almost crying, he wanted to go so bad. So I figured why not let him just as long as he promised to come right back and not go off the block? Besides, I told my boyfriend where I was sitting tonight and he called on the phone right in the middle of all this going on, so—"

"You mean you disobeyed our orders?" There was no slur in Irene's voice now, only the sharp shrill of sudden anger. "You let him go?"

"I'm sorry. I guess I wasn't thinking—"

"Never mind that." Howard's hoarse voice held apprehension as well as anger. "How long ago was this?"

"How long?" Connie shook her head. "I don't know. I mean, I was on the phone and then I started playing the stereo, like maybe around ten o'clock."

"Then he's been gone over an hour." Howard's face was grim. "Maybe an hour and a half, while you sat there blabbing with your boyfriend and listening to that goddamn rock crap!"

Connie began to cry, but Irene ignored her. She turned to her husband. "Why don't you get in the car and take a run around the block? He can't have gone very far."

"I hope to God you're right." Howard moved toward the hall. "Meanwhile, you better phone the Summerses and see if Bill brought him back over there."

"Good idea. I never thought of that." Irene was already dialing as Howard started up the car outside, and she could hear it pulling away as Mrs. Summers responded to her call.

"Hello—Midge?" Irene spoke quickly. "Sorry to bother you at this late hour, but I was wondering—"

Connie stood beside her, trying to control her sniffles as she listened. But Irene's words and the pauses between them told their own story, and when at last she hung up and turned her anguished face to the light Connie started to cry again.

"You heard?" Irene said. "Bill's gone too." Then her voice broke. "Oh my God!" She rose. "What's keeping Howard so long?"

The answer came as a car screeched to a halt in the driveway and Irene opened the front door to admit her husband. The night wind was cold, but what really chilled her as he entered was the realization that Howard was alone.

"No sign of him," he muttered. "I covered everything for a half mile up and down, and there's not a kid out anywhere."

"There wouldn't be, at this hour." Irene nodded. "I know he's not at the Summerses', but maybe he and Bill stopped by somewhere else. I'm going to phone the Coopers and see—"

"Don't bother," Howard said. "I've just come from there. And before that I looked in on the Stuttmans and those new people, Higgins or whatever their name is. Their kids haven't come home either."

"But that's impossible! Do you realize it's past eleven-thirty?" She trembled, fighting the tears. "Where could they be?"

"We'll find out." Howard brushed past her, striding toward the phone. "I'm calling the police."

The grandfather's clock began to boom its message of midnight as potbellied Benjamin Franklin and little old Mrs. See peered into the parlor at the left of the front hallway.

"I'm glad we used candy this time," she said. "And that was a good idea of yours, giving money instead if the youngsters came to the door with their parents."

It was dark in the parlor and they had only a moment to stare through the shadows at the huddled forms lying motionless within.

"How many are there?" he said.

"Thirteen." She beamed at him as the chimes came to an end. "At least we won't be going hungry."

Sergeant Lichner kept his cool, but it wasn't easy. The station was like a madhouse, all those parents yelling and crying, and it took a team of four men just to question them and get some facts, instead of listening to wild guesses about kidnappers or crazies who put razor blades in Halloween candy.

But in the end he got it all together, using the statements to map out a route. Putting through some phone calls to establish where each child or group of children had last been seen, it turned out that everything must have happened somewhere within the area of one square block.

Then he called in backups and started out. There were four black-and-whites assigned to the search, each with its quota of parents, and each taking a single side of the block as they went from door to door asking questions.

On three sides the answers formed a pattern. Various youngsters had knocked on doors at various times, but all had been seen and accounted for.

Sergeant Lichner himself was in a fifth car, and to speed matters up he took one end of the block while the fourth car started at the other.

It wasn't until the two cars converged in the middle of the block to compare notes that he got an answer. Sid Olney pulled up and got out, shaking his head. "They were here, all right," he said. "Stopped at every house back there, right on up until around eleven. What did you find out, anything?"

Sergeant Lichner took a deep breath. "Same as you." He glanced at the house directly behind him. "Folks in the last place said the Esterhazy kid and the Summers boy were there late, almost eleven-thirty. What time did your people see them?"

Sid Olney shook his head. "They didn't." He shook his head. "That's funny."

But there was no mirth in his eyes, or the eyes of the parents as they stared at the spot where the trail ended—the space between the two houses looming on either side of the weed-choked vacant lot lying empty and deserted under the Halloween moon.